"Go back inside."

"No, David. I intend to stay with you." Elizabeth gripped the back of his coat.

There wasn't time to argue. He carefully descended the cellar stairs, using the lantern to illuminate the area.

When he reached the bottom, he swept the light in a complete circle, but no one was there.

His gaze landed on the puddles of water on the floor.

"Someone was here," Elizabeth whispered.

"Yes." He slowly straightened and once again swept the lantern over the area.

Without warning, the cellar door slammed shut. He lunged up the stairs to stop it, but it was too late.

He pushed against the door, expecting it to open, but it didn't move.

Panic gripped him by the throat. He pushed again, using all his strength. The door moved a fraction of an inch, but no farther.

The wind hadn't closed the cellar doors, but someone had.

They were trapped.

Laura Scott has always loved romance and read faith-based books by Grace Livingston Hill in her teenage years. She's thrilled to have been given the opportunity to retire from thirty-eight years of nursing to become a full-time author. Laura has published over thirty books for Love Inspired Suspense. She has two adult children and lives in Milwaukee, Wisconsin, with her husband of thirty-five years. Please visit Laura at laurascottbooks.com, as she loves to hear from her readers.

Books by Laura Scott

Love Inspired Suspense

Hiding in Plain Sight
Amish Holiday Vendetta

Justice Seekers

Soldier's Christmas Secrets
Guarded by the Soldier
Wyoming Mountain Escape
Hiding His Holiday Witness
Rocky Mountain Standoff
Fugitive Hunt

Rocky Mountain K-9 Unit

Hiding in Montana

Visit the Author Profile page at LoveInspired.com for more titles.

Amish Holiday Vendetta

Laura Scott

LOVE INSPIRED SUSPENSE
INSPIRATIONAL ROMANCE

LOVE INSPIRED® SUSPENSE
INSPIRATIONAL ROMANCE

Recycling programs
for this product may
not exist in your area.

ISBN-13: 978-1-335-58811-1

Amish Holiday Vendetta

Copyright © 2022 by Laura Iding

For questions and comments about the quality of this book, please contact us
at CustomerService@Harlequin.com.

Love Inspired
22 Adelaide St. West, 41st Floor
Toronto, Ontario M5H 4E3, Canada
www.LoveInspired.com

Printed in U.S.A.

O taste and see that the Lord is good:
blessed is the man that trusteth in him.
—*Psalm* 34:8

This book is dedicated with love to
Sally Nowak and Vicki Christman, two of my biggest fans.
I'm truly blessed to have wonderful readers like you!

ONE

Elizabeth Walton battled a wave of apprehension as she walked home from the Amish Shoppe in Green Lake, Wisconsin, where she sold her handmade quilts. She shouldn't have lingered for so long. Darkness came early in mid-December, and there was a dusting of fresh snow covering the ground, making some areas slick. Part of her dread was knowing *Mammi* Ruth would once again express how Elizabeth had failed her husband. Ruth's son, Adam, had died six months ago after a terrible fall, and *Mammi* Ruth continued to treat Elizabeth with disdain, placing the fault with her. As if she had somehow caused Adam to tumble from the loft and land on the floor of the barn, hitting his head with such force as to cause massive bleeding into his brain.

And mayhap there was blame to share, as deep down, Elizabeth knew she hadn't loved

Adam the way she should have. It had been a marriage arranged by the elders, and one that she had not wanted. Yet she had done her duty to Adam for the two years they were married. She still prayed for God's forgiveness for feeling nothing but relief after Adam had passed away.

The hoot of an owl startled her. She shot a quick glance over her shoulder, but the road behind her remained empty of traffic. For the past few days, Elizabeth had the uneasy feeling of being watched. And just last night, she'd caught a glimpse of someone lurking near the barn, which was no longer in use.

She'd told herself to stop imagining things, as there would be no reason for anyone to go the empty barn. Young teens, maybe, looking for a place to meet, but they tended to hang out in groups, not individually.

And not at such a late hour in mid-December.

As she approached the entrance to her home, her footsteps instinctively slowed while she searched for a sign that someone might be lurking nearby. Was it her imagination? Or was someone moving along the right side of her house?

"Who's there?" she called sharply. "Show yourself!"

No response.

A shiver that had nothing to do with the cold winter air rippled over her. She clutched her cape close and quickened her pace, taking care not to slip on the snow-covered ground. The front door was close now. If she could just get inside…

This time, she heard a thudding sound coming from the side of the house where the shadow had been.

Someone was there! Steeling her resolve, Elizabeth forced herself to investigate. Mayhap the three Johannesburg boys were seeking to play tricks on her.

"Who's there?" she called again. "Benjamin Johannesburg, is that you? Are your brothers here, too?"

Still no response, but as she peered around the corner, there was no mistaking the trail of footprints in the snow leading away from her house and toward the barn.

One set of footprints, not three.

Fear closed around her throat, choking her, but she forced herself to be strong as she followed the prints all the way to the barn. She hadn't been inside since the fateful day Adam had fallen to his death.

She shivered again when she saw the sliding door was open just a few inches. Not wide enough for someone to get in and out, but surely an indication that someone had been there recently. Especially given the fresh footprints in the snow. Using caution, she approached the door and called again, "Who is in there? Please show yourself!"

The darkness made it impossible to see man or beast, although the livestock had been taken by the elders after Adam's death to be used for the good of the community. She shoved at the door, opening it wider. A musty, stale scent wafted toward her.

She hesitated, her feet refusing to take her inside. What if the intruder was waiting for the chance to lash out against her? She couldn't imagine why anyone would do such a thing, but the fresh set of footprints in the snow was proof someone had sought shelter there.

"If you're cold, you are welcome to come to the house." She made the offer in case the intruder was a stranger to the area and had nowhere else to go. After several long moments, with no response, she turned away. A small kerosene lantern flickered from *Mammi* Ruth's bedroom window. Her mother-in-law was no doubt becoming impatient, waiting for Elizabeth to return. Even though *Mammi* Ruth was physically able to perform some basic cooking and cleaning, she tended to allow Elizabeth to do the work, expecting to be waited upon.

She was halfway to the house when she heard the crunching sound of boots against the snow. She turned just as a pair of hands struck hard in the center of her back. The momentum sent her sprawling to the ground, her palms and knees stinging with pain, her face planted in the thin layer of snow.

Stunned, she didn't move for a long moment, hardly able to comprehend what had just happened. Then she quickly pushed to her feet, swiping the snow from her face. She raked her gaze over the area, searching for whoever had done such a mean thing. More footprints were visible in the snow, leading through the yard and disappearing in a wooded area that separated her property from her neighbor next door.

Her shoulders slumped as she realized her attacker was gone.

Doing her best to ignore the pain in her hands, knees and chin, Elizabeth headed to the back door, questions swirling in her mind.

The assault didn't make any sense. The Amish community was close-knit, and the members always helped each other in times of need. The elders made sure everyone was cared for, and physical violence was not tolerated. Bishop Bachman's sermons supported these beliefs.

Not only had someone sneaked around her house and hidden in her barn, but they'd attacked her from behind, no doubt to distract her so they could escape without being caught.

Who would do such a thing? And why?

Elizabeth had no idea.

Yet she was very much afraid this wasn't an isolated event. That whoever had been there would return.

And next time, the assailant may try something far more sinister than simply pushing her to the ground.

David McKay had developed the bad habit of staying late at the Amish Shoppe. He'd closed his storefront at the same time all the other shop owners did, as the main doors of the renovated barn were locked at the end of the day. The Amish Shoppe housed several Amish businesses. But he was one of the few vendors who had enough space to house his workroom behind his showroom. Since there was no one waiting for him in his dark, empty house, he often worked late, choosing to sleep on the cot he'd set up in his small kitchenette.

Tonight he'd stayed up to finish a baby cradle. In the past few months, it had become his hottest-selling item. He carried the cradle into the front showroom and set it in a prominent location right in front of the door to draw attention. He made a mental note to ask Elizabeth for one of her baby quilts to put on display the following morning. Elizabeth Walton had a quilt shop right next to his showroom, and they often joined forces to market each other's wares.

Just thinking of Elizabeth made him smile. They were only friends, but that didn't stop him from secretly longing for more.

Unfortunately, she didn't know anything about his checkered past, especially the four years he'd spent in jail for manslaughter. She was also an Amish widow, and the Amish didn't readily welcome outsiders into their community. David had changed his ways after being released from prison. He'd done his best to mold his life after the Amish, choosing to give up electricity, cars, power tools and other modern technology the way the Amish did, but he knew that alone wasn't enough.

A flash of movement at the far end of the Amish Shoppe caught his eye. He frowned and moved closer to the glass doors that ran along the front of his showroom. It was unusual for one of the other Amish shop owners to be here so late, nearly nine o'clock on this Wednesday night, but he couldn't imagine who else would be there. The front doors of the Amish Shoppe were locked, so anyone coming in would need a key.

A short, dark shadow moved from one side of the main aisle to the other. The tiny hairs on the back of David's neck lifted in warning. Without hesitation, he quickly unlocked his showroom door and soundlessly pushed it open. He moved down the row of shops to his right, staying on the opposite side of where he'd seen the shadow.

He belatedly realized he should have grabbed the cell phone he'd recently acquired, but the thought hadn't occurred to him. He and Elizabeth shared the device, having been granted permission from the Amish elders to use it for business purposes.

Reporting a man lurking in the shop wasn't exactly business related. Unless he was there to rob the place.

David moved silently along the hallway, his keen gaze trying to find the shadow. It occurred to him that one of the Amish members would have simply gone straight to their shop.

The shadow moved again.

"Who's there?" His voice echoed along the long center aisle.

Something hit the floor with a loud crash. Then the shadow ran, heading toward the main doorway. David quickly followed.

"Stop! Who are you? What do you want?"

The guy wrenched open the door, then turned back. When David saw the gun in the short, burly man's hand, he hit the ground just as the pistol boomed sharply and the bullet whizzed by.

What was going on?

David gingerly lifted his head, only to realize the guy had vanished. He jumped to his feet and ran outside. But it was too late. He heard the rumble of a car engine, the taillights quickly disappearing from his line of sight.

David blew out a breath, trying to calm his racing heart. He turned to head back inside, then paused and crouched down to examine the main doors. There were tiny scratches in the metal around the lock.

Lockpick tools had been used to access the building by a man with a gun.

Why? To commit a robbery? It was possible, as the Amish were known to favor cash transactions over credit cards. Yet the Amish were also smart enough to take their proceeds home with them each night. In the eighteen months he'd been there, the Amish Shoppe had never been targeted by thieves. The Green Lake area didn't have a lot of crime.

Well, not until a few months ago, when he and his niece, Shauna, had been targeted by several bad guys. But that was a once-in-a life-time event.

Wasn't it?

After heading inside, David made sure to lock the main doors again, before examining the area. He found the source of the crash to be a small rack of scented, Christmas candles in red and green, now sprawled on the floor outside Clara's Candle Shoppe.

Thankfully, only one of them had been broken. He righted the rack and replaced the candles, tucking money beneath the one that was broken. Then his gaze dropped to the wooden plank floor, noting there were several wet spots left behind by the intruder. There had been a dusting of snow outside, and the gunman had tracked some of that snow in on his feet.

David walked the entire interior of the Amish Shoppe, just to be sure he didn't miss anything else. He'd only seen one man, but there could have been more.

But the place was empty except for him. David assumed the way he'd called out had scared the guy into running.

The intruder hadn't expected anyone to be here. Logically, that tipped the scales toward the motive being a robbery, but David couldn't quite make himself believe it. Mostly because of the way the guy had aimed his weapon directly at him and fired.

Wouldn't the average robber have just run off without shooting?

A shiver snaked down his spine as he returned to his showroom. He made sure to lock the door before heading into the work area in the back. He unplugged the phone from its charger and stared at the screen. Then he set it aside. He knew the Amish community preferred to solve their differences among themselves, rather than involving outsiders like the police.

Green Lake County Sheriff Liam Harland had married his niece, Shauna, last month. Technically that made David Liam's uncle, although they were only about eight years apart in age. He was torn between being true to the Amish lifestyle he'd chosen and knowing Liam should be aware of what had happened here tonight.

Maybe he'd call in the morning. No reason

to wake Liam and Shauna this late. The intruder was gone, and thankfully nothing had been stolen.

The wind picked up outside. The small woodburning stove didn't always heat up the large area. Normally, the physical effort of creating furniture helped keep him warm, but not as much when he stretched out on the cot, even with the comfort of huddling beneath two of Elizabeth's thick quilts.

David fell into a restless sleep, fragmented dreams keeping him on edge. The mistakes he'd made in the past had intermingled with the gunman who'd entered the Amish Shoppe. This time, the gunman found him and shot directly at his chest. David woke up just before he felt the impact of the bullet.

Sweat dampened his brow despite the chill in the air. He drew in a deep breath to ground himself, then crawled from the cot to add wood to the stove.

Using an old-fashioned percolator on his woodstove, he made coffee. His stomach rumbled with hunger. He sat at his small table and bowed his head. He prayed for God to bless his food, and to keep the Amish Shoppe safe from further criminal activity. Then he finished the small amount of bread and cheese left over from last night's dinner. It wasn't enough to fill him up, but when the Amish Shoppe opened for business, he'd walk down to the Sunshine Café for breakfast. Elizabeth sometimes joined him, and while he knew they could only be friends, sharing meals with her was the highlight of his day.

Being just over a week from Christmas brought more customers to the Amish Shoppe than usual. Come January, the crowds would be thin. The Amish didn't decorate their homes the way the English did for the holiday, but they did weave some Christmas themes into their wares this time of the year.

He enjoyed the holiday spirit. He strode down the center aisle, then abruptly stopped when he thought about the events of the night before.

Where was the bullet?

He went to the spot where he'd been standing and looked around. Judging by where the shooter had been standing, he followed the most logical trajectory, leading back behind him. The center aisle was long and narrow, with his showroom located at the end.

He returned to his showroom. The glass doors were still intact, which made sense as he'd left them open when he'd gone after the intruder. Yet as he looked more closely at the baby cradle he'd just finished, he saw it.

A small bullet hole in the side. An ugly display of violence in a cradle that was meant to surround a new arrival with love.

He fought a wave of despair. He was thankful that he hadn't been injured, but he obviously couldn't sell the cradle now. He carried it back to his showroom. It was something to show Liam later.

Pushing aside the grim thoughts, he walked to the Sunshine Café. Leah Moore smiled shyly and gestured for him to have a seat. She ran the café on the days the shops were open. "The usual, David?"

"Yes, please." He glanced over toward the main entrance. "Did Elizabeth come with you this morning?"

"She did, *ja*." Leah's smile faded. "She ducked into the restroom."

Before he could say anything more, Elizabeth came toward him. He frowned and jumped to his feet when he saw the abrasion on her chin, and the way she was favoring her left side.

"What happened?"

"*Ach*, 'tis nothing." Elizabeth avoided his direct gaze as she eased into the seat across the small table.

"You're hurt." David had worked hard over the years to hold his temper in check, so he did his best to keep his tone even. "Did something happen on your way home last evening? You should have allowed me to accompany you."

"I slipped and fell in the snow." She turned and glanced at Leah, who was watching them closely. "I'll have my usual eggs, toast and jam, *ja*?"

"Sehr gut." Leah nodded. After a moment's hesitation, the girl moved away to make their meals.

"Are you sure this is nothing more than a slip and fall?" David pressed. There was something off about the way Elizabeth was acting. Normally, if she'd done something silly, she'd laugh it off.

"Why do you ask?" Her sharp tone was unlike her.

"Because I care, Elizabeth." He reached over to lightly touch the back of her hand, hoping to reassure her. "I hope you know you can come to me if you need help."

She lifted her head to look at him, and the anguish in her brown eyes ripped at his heart. *"Denke*, David. I do know—" She abruptly stopped speaking, the blood draining from her face.

"What is it?" He turned in his seat to see an Amish man roughly David's age of thirty-six striding toward them. He wore a long coat, a hat and gloves. The man's gaze was centered on Elizabeth. Instantly, she removed her hand from his, hiding it in her lap.

"Elizabeth." The man completely ignored David. "I was surprised to learn you didn't wait for me this morning. You were told I'd be giving you a ride today in my buggy, *ja*?"

Elizabeth lifted her chin. "*Ach*, I'm sorry, Jacob. *Mammi* Ruth woke earlier than usual. I must have misjudged the time."

The man's gaze bored into her with such intensity that David had to force himself to remain seated, rather than jumping to his feet and stepping between them. He knew Elizabeth well enough to understand she hadn't forgotten but had deliberately left home early enough to avoid riding with this guy.

For a moment he wondered if Jacob was the gunman he'd run into during the middle of the night. But then he dismissed the thought. Jacob was too tall to be the intruder he'd seen. Besides, a man who wanted to court a woman did not break into the Amish Shoppe with lockpick tools and a handgun.

Yet the tension between the two couldn't

be ignored. The urge to come to Elizabeth's defense was strong. And all too reminiscent of the way he'd gotten into trouble helping Amanda all those years ago. While he'd started off with good intentions back then, his actions had cost a man his life. And sent David to jail for manslaughter.

Violence doesn't solve anything, he reminded himself. *Jesus taught us to turn the other cheek.*

"Well, then, I shall see you this evening," Jacob said in a tone that did not invite argument. "I will be here at quarter past five o'clock to drive you home."

Elizabeth didn't respond, which only seemed to irritate the man. After a prolonged, heavy silence, Jacob finally turned and walked away.

"Elizabeth, why is Jacob so intent on driving you back and forth? What's going on?"

She slowly shook her head, her expression grim. "*Ach*, David, I don't know why he has taken this approach. Jacob Strauss is an old friend of my husband, but I've made it clear I'm not interested. Unfortunately, many of the elders offer rides to and from work as they're able to assist, so I believe he feels I should be accepting a ride with him the same way."

"I'll walk you home," he quickly offered. "There's no reason for you to go with him."

"Denke." Her swift agreement only caused him to worry more. Clearly, she wanted to avoid Jacob's company. But even worse was the stark fear that lingered in her wide brown eyes.

Something was wrong. Very wrong. Too bad, she didn't yet trust him enough to share what it was.

TWO

Elizabeth gripped her hands tightly to hide the trembling from David's keen gaze. The fear she'd felt last night after being ruthlessly shoved to the ground had returned full force, the moment she'd seen Jacob striding toward her.

He may have been close to Adam, but he was no friend of hers.

She'd never cared for him even back when she and Adam had been married. The man had rarely smiled and his tone was always tense and authoritarian. Her disdain for him had only gotten worse after Jacob inappropriately approached her a mere two weeks after Adam's death, bluntly stating he had chosen to court her. He hadn't asked, or even hinted that her opinion mattered in the least. Irritated, she'd politely refused, but when he persisted, she'd taken her concerns to Bishop Bachman. The bishop was very understanding and had immediately spoken to Jacob, reminding him of the proper mourning period and that Elizabeth had the right to choose her suitor. Jacob had appeared angry about what she'd done, but he'd left her alone.

Until recently. The past couple of days he'd been pressing to spend time with her, hence these constant offers to drive her to and from the Amish Shoppe. It had been fine when the Amish elders had done so, because they performed the task out of respect for her status as a widow. But she didn't trust Jacob's intentions and had absolutely no interest in being on the receiving end of his attention.

Jacob had married his wife, Anna, several years before she and Adam had wed. Roughly nine months before Adam's death, Anna and their son, Isaac, had died in a tragic buggy accident. There had been rumblings about Anna's intent to leave her husband, since the buggy had been found far from their Amish community. And there had been whispers about Jacob's tendency to lash out in anger.

Mammi Ruth spoke harshly against the gossip, supporting Jacob and Adam as good men of their Amish community. Elizabeth wasn't convinced, at least as far as Adam was concerned, but held her tongue. Her relationship with *Mammi* Ruth was strained enough. There was no reason to make it worse.

"I wish you would trust me enough to confide your troubles." David's low, husky voice interrupted her thoughts. "I'm here for you, Elizabeth."

His offer was sweet and she forced herself to shake off the impending sense of doom. The assault late last evening still bothered her, but she did her best to downplay the event. Surely if the attacker had wanted to hurt her, he would have done more than shove her to the ground. "*Denke*, but truly there's nothing to worry about. *Ach*, here comes Leah with our breakfast."

After Leah had set their plates on the table, David bowed his head. She was touched by the way David always included her in his prayers.

"Dear Lord, we ask You to bless this food You have provided for us. We also ask that You heal Elizabeth's injures while keeping her safe in Your care, amen."

"Amen," she whispered.

The food was wonderful as always, and she watched beneath her lashes as David enjoyed his meal. He was handsome, kind and gentle. He was an *Englischer*, but one who valued the simple life of the Amish. Many tourists were curious about their lifestyle, but none had embraced it the way David McKay had. Each workday she looked forward to spending time with him. Unfortunately, the Amish Shoppe had shorter hours over the long winter months when tourism was scarce, which meant she saw him less often. On the days the shops were closed, she missed their time together, far more than she should.

She valued David's friendship more than anything. Mayhap if things were different…

No, there was no point in yearning for something she couldn't have. *Mammi* Ruth was difficult enough, adding an *Englischer* to the mix would make the situation unbearable. Besides, Elizabeth did not plan to marry, ever again.

"I can tell something is troubling you," David said.

He was far too good at reading her moods. She finished her eggs and pushed her empty plate aside. "I've been trying to come up with a way to avoid returning home with Jacob. I know you offered to escort me today, but I sense he'll only try again."

"I'll escort you home every night," David said firmly. "No reason for you to ride with him." There was a brief pause before he added, "It appears Jacob seeks to court you."

She frowned. "I have made it clear I am not interested. Bishop Bachman has supported my decision."

The tension around David's mouth relaxed. "I understand, especially since you are still in mourning."

"My marriage to Adam was not a love match." The truth tumbled boldly from her lips, before she could stop it. It was a fact few people knew, and one of the reasons their bishop supported her decision to remain unmarried now.

"I see." David's frown indicated otherwise. "I appreciate you telling me."

Her cheeks warmed. "I only mention it so you understand that my reluctance to see Jacob has nothing to do with mourning my husband. I don't care for Jacob, it's true, but I also have no interest in marrying again. Ever."

A flash of emotion darkened David's blue gaze, but it was gone so quickly she assumed she'd imagined it. "That certainly clarifies things," he said quietly.

Leah returned to clear their plates. David quickly paid Leah for their meals, shaking his head when Elizabeth offered to pay her own way.

He walked with her to the quilt shop located right next to his furniture store. She'd been blessed to have the ability to showcase some of her quilts in his woodworking shop. David had confessed that his baby cradle was now his bestselling item, and she was pleased to have played a role in that.

The same way her baby quilts and marriage quilts had become her highest-selling items. Two things that were sought after by many, but not her.

A family of her own was not part of God's plan for her.

"I will see you later, Elizabeth."

"Sehr gut," she murmured in agreement, watching as he turned away.

She'd recently made several quilts with a cheery Christmas theme of reds and greens, though nothing showy, as that wasn't their way. The customers loved them. As the day progressed, her limp became more pronounced due to the swelling in her left knee. Just as she was beginning to close her shop, she noticed that Shauna and Liam had come by to visit David. Liam was her cousin—their mothers were sisters—but Liam's parents had left the Amish community when he was young. Yet family was important and she was grateful to see him on a regular basis. She locked her door, wincing at the realization that walking home with her sore knee would be a challenge.

Still, she'd rather walk with David than ride with Jacob.

She hovered near David's door, watching as Liam, Shauna and David spoke. Whatever the conversation was about, it seemed rather intense. It might be something important, and she didn't want to intrude. After another five minutes passed, she told herself not to be foolish. She headed outside, breathing a sigh of relief that Jacob wasn't already there waiting for her.

God was watching over her, she thought. Setting out at a brisk pace while ignoring the pain in her knee, she hoped Jacob had gotten tied up with his chores taking care of the livestock. She was certain she could make it all the way home before he came looking for her. Knowing him, he'd assume she'd wait.

Mayhap she would wait for David, but never for Jacob.

The clippety-clop of hooves on pavement brought a wave of dread. She could see the buggy approaching along the road, and her entire body tensed when she recognized Jacob as the buggy driver. She almost groaned out loud.

Ignoring him, she continued walking. Even when the buggy pulled alongside her, she didn't turn to look at him.

"Stop, Elizabeth. I'm here to drive you home," Jacob said in that arrogant, bossy tone she despised.

She shook her head, avoiding his direct gaze. "*Denke,* but I prefer to walk. It's better to sustain health, ain't so?"

"Don't be foolish, it's too cold to walk." His tone was dismissive. She ground her teeth, not caring for his attitude.

"I'm fine."

"Get in," Jacob said firmly. "I came all this way for you."

As if she'd asked him to. Her scowl deepened. This stretch of road was deserted, making her feel isolated and vulnerable. She wished now that she had waited for David to accompany her. Elizabeth quickened her pace, which didn't help since the horse could easily outrun her.

"Elizabeth? Wait up, you forgot your scarf." David's voice came from behind her. Overwhelmed with relief, she looked back to see him running along the side of the road to catch up. In his hand, he carried a length of fabric that must have fallen out of her pocket at one point. It wasn't a scarf, but she was tempted to smile as Jacob wouldn't know the difference.

"*Denke.*" She took several steps forward,

meeting him halfway. The concern in his eyes warmed her heart.

"Elizabeth, there's a customer back at the Amish Shoppe requesting to speak to you about one of your quilts. I know we're officially closed, but she was very insistent."

Lying was a sin, but she played along. "*Ach*, of course I should meet with her."

"I'll be happy to escort you back to the Amish Shoppe," David offered.

"I'll drive you," Jacob said loudly from the buggy.

"*Ach*, no, I couldn't trouble you so, Jacob. Best that you return home to take care of the animals, *ja*?" She barely looked at him.

"Do not just walk away from me," Jacob said in a low voice.

The implied threat spurred her ire. She spun to face him, locking her gaze on his. "Or what? You'll do me harm? Mayhap push me to the ground? Or something worse?"

Anger flashed in his eyes, but then he looked concerned. "What? No. Of course, not. I would never hurt you."

"*Sehr gut.*" She turned back toward David, who warily watched the exchange. "*Komm.* We must hurry."

David took her hand in his, and despite

the way they were both wearing gloves, the warmth of his palm shimmered all the way up her arm.

They'd gone several yards before the horse's hooves pounded the pavement as Jacob finally gave up and headed home.

"I don't like his persistence." David broke the silence between them once the buggy was out of sight.

"*Ja*, I feel the same." There was no reason to believe Jacob had been the one lurking near her house, hiding in the barn and then assaulting her. It didn't make any sense for him to do those things if he indeed wanted to court her.

Somehow, she couldn't shake the idea that Jacob was a potential source of danger.

A man she needed to avoid at all costs.

Twice now, David had had to rein in his temper when it came to Jacob's interactions with Elizabeth.

Not good.

He had prayed all day for patience and perseverance. That God would continue guiding him down His chosen path. Granting David the peace and forgiveness he sought.

Yet just hearing the way Jacob spoke to Elizabeth set his teeth on edge. The man was too high-handed, a trait he rarely encountered during his interactions with other Amish men within the community.

He wished Jacob was the gunman, since he'd like nothing more than to send Liam after him, but Jacob was much taller than the attacker he'd chased off.

"*Denke*, David. *Sehr gut* of you to come for me."

"You should have waited," he chided gently. "I promised to escort you home."

She nodded. "*Ja*, I waited a bit, but I didn't want to interrupt your time with Shauna and Liam."

"It wasn't family time, Elizabeth." He hesitated, then decided she should know the truth. "There was an incident last night in the Amish Shoppe that I needed to discuss with Liam."

"What kind of incident?"

"A man picked the lock on the front door and was moving around inside. When I called out to him, he ran, stopping just long enough to shoot at me." He kept his voice even. "The bullet is lodged in the baby cradle I'd just finished. Liam took the bullet remnant away for evidence."

"No!" She turned to stare at him. "He shot

at you. That's terrible! Who would do such a thing?"

"I don't know. But it's possible he intended to steal items or cash." He shrugged. "The gunman was shorter than Jacob, so I don't believe he's involved. But we must be on alert for anything suspicious."

"I understand," she murmured.

He held her hand as they made a circle in the road to head toward her house. Thankfully, Jacob's buggy was now out of sight. "Liam is going to see if there have been any other reports of armed robberies in the area." He hesitated, then added, "You need to take care, Elizabeth. No more leaving on your own without me. Walking home alone in the dark isn't smart." Especially not with a man like Jacob lurking nearby, he thought grimly.

"*Ja*, I agree." She tightened her grip on his hand. "Well, there are only two more days left to work, Friday and Saturday. After that, the shops will be closed until the following Wednesday. I won't be on the road, then, *ja*?"

"Yes." The shorter workweek was due to the lack of tourists coming to Green Lake this time of year. He tried to use the extra time to build his inventory, but he truly missed seeing

Elizabeth for those days the shops were closed. "Will you be okay at home alone?"

She didn't answer, her gaze seemingly focused on something off in the distance. He tried to see what had captured her attention, but it was only her house.

"Elizabeth?" he prompted.

"What? *Ach*, yes. I shall be fine." The words were meant to reassure, yet her voice lacked conviction.

They continued walking. From here, he could see a light shining from one of the windows of her home. "How are things going with your mother-in-law?"

She shrugged. "The same. She grieves the loss of her son."

That wasn't a reason to treat Elizabeth poorly, but he didn't voice his opinion. Elizabeth would not be swayed from doing her duty, caring for her mother-in-law even after working all day at the quilt shop.

They walked the rest of the way in silence. Upon reaching her front door, he released her hand and stepped back. "Good night, Elizabeth."

She used her key to unlock the door, then suddenly turned to him. "David, would you care to stay for dinner?"

Her invitation was so unexpected he could only gape at her. "I—uh, thought your mother-in-law wouldn't approve?"

"Mayhap that is true, but I should still like you to stay. I have leftover beef roast and butternut squash soup," she added with a grin.

His stomach growled with anticipation. "I would love to join you, as long as my doing so doesn't cause more trouble for you."

"It won't." Again, her tone lacked conviction. David had escorted Elizabeth home on many occasions but had never stepped foot inside her house. He did so now, glancing around with curiosity. To his surprise the stark interior was warmly inviting. There was a hint of cinnamon in the air, a scent he often associated with her.

"I need to check on *Mammi* Ruth." Elizabeth hung her cloak on a peg, then slid off her boots. "Please make yourself comfortable."

The embers were low in the woodburning stove. "I'll feed the fire."

She smiled at his offer, then hurried off. Listening to the muted voices coming from the second floor, he took a moment to add wood to the stove, hoping the conversation wasn't too contentious. When that was finished, he headed back outside to the woodpile to bring in more firewood. He stacked the wood as high as he could, hoping to provide enough to last her over the next several days.

He told himself not to get used to performing these sorts of tasks for Elizabeth, as this invitation wasn't likely to be repeated anytime soon. Especially knowing her mother-in-law disapproved.

By the time he'd finished stacking wood, Elizabeth had warmed up their meal. Her mother-in-law was seated at the kitchen table, glaring at Elizabeth as she moved around the kitchen.

"*Mammi* Ruth, I would like you to meet my friend David McKay. He is a furniture maker and sells his goods in the store next to my quilt shop." Elizabeth forced a smile. "David, this is *Mammi* Ruth Walton."

"Pleased to meet you," David said.

"Bah, *Englischer*," she spat. His gaze widened as Ruth continued in Pennsylvania Dutch, a language he only partially understood. By the flicker of anger in Elizabeth's eyes it was obvious her comments were not very nice.

"David was kind enough to walk me home and to stack firewood for us. Sharing our dinner is the least I can do," Elizabeth said firmly. "Now please, allow me to say grace."

He bowed his head and listened intently. Elizabeth recited the prayer in Pennsylvania Dutch for *Mammi* Ruth's benefit, then repeated it in English. The elder woman didn't look happy, but she accepted the basket of bread Elizabeth handed to her, reluctantly passing it along to him.

Despite the strained atmosphere, the food was delicious. When Elizabeth's mother-in-law was finished eating, Elizabeth jumped up to escort her back to her room. The older woman didn't bother to bid him good-night.

While they were gone, David quickly stacked the dirty dishes in the sink. He was about to begin washing them when he glimpsed movement through the kitchen window.

Was someone out there?

The memory of the gunman turning to fire at him flashed in his mind. David quickly crossed to the door. He took a moment to shrug into his coat before heading outside. The wind wasn't as brisk as the night before, but the single-digit temperatures stole his breath.

He stayed close to the side of the house, only detouring around the cellar doors, hoping to blend into the shadows. As he went around the corner, he frowned when he saw partially filled footprints in the snow.

Remembering how Elizabeth had mentioned slipping and falling, he relaxed, realizing they were hers.

Only they weren't. Upon closer inspection, he found two sets of footprints, a large pair and a small pair.

A man and a woman? A shaft of anger hit hard. It was all too easy to imagine Jacob being out there, stalking Elizabeth.

He flexed his fingers, reminding himself that violence didn't solve anything. He'd learned his lesson, had sought God's love and understanding to prevent himself from allowing anger to overwhelm him ever again.

As he continued moving around the house, he noticed the dual sets of footprints leading all the way to the barn. He found that odd, considering Elizabeth had told him a few months ago she didn't house any livestock.

There was also a large area of disturbed snow halfway between the house and the barn. From that location, the smaller set of footprints crossed the yard away from the barn, heading to the house. Interesting. Elizabeth must have fallen here, then headed back inside.

The area didn't look particularly icy, though. A fact that gave him pause.

His gaze swept around the area again, landing on the open barn door. He quickly strode toward it. If nothing else, he would close it up tight to prevent animals like coyotes, raccoons and other scavengers from getting inside.

As he poked his head through the doorway, the musty scent made him sneeze. He couldn't see much of anything through the darkness, which was why he was caught off guard when a rough hand grabbed his coat and dragged him forward into the dark interior.

His old fighting instincts rose to the surface. He lashed out with his foot, causing the person to grunt in pain as he hit something solid. He swung with his fist but found nothing but air.

Where was the assailant? In his mind's eye David imagined Jacob hiding inside, determined to take him out of the picture.

Something hard crashed against his head. Blinding pain reverberated through his temple, sending him down to the floor in a crumpled heap.

Then there was nothing but darkness.

THREE

Elizabeth had known *Mammi* Ruth wouldn't approve of David staying for dinner, but she didn't care. Ignoring her mother-in-law was easy. She let every complaint the woman uttered go without offering an argument in return. There was no point, since the woman held her opinions like a shield to her chest. Elizabeth did her duty caring for her husband's mother, and wasn't that enough?

Besides, after being shoved to the ground the evening before, she'd felt better having David stay, even for a short time. And his taking over the chore of bringing in the firewood without being asked had been kind.

It had been a long time since she'd felt cared for.

But even though Elizabeth enjoyed David's company, she hadn't been lying when she told him she wasn't interested in being married again. For one thing, she hadn't enjoyed being married the first time. And she preferred making her own decisions rather than being told what to do. She was happy having her freedom, as much as she had while still caring for *Mammi* Ruth.

Her quilt shop was far more successful than she could have ever hoped. God has blessed her with a skill that provided food and other necessities. Anything extra that was not needed, she gave to the rest of the community, as was the Amish way.

When she finished with *Mammi* Ruth, she returned to the kitchen. Their supper dishes were neatly stacked in the sink, but there was no sign of David.

She frowned, noting his coat and boots were missing from the peg near the door. Had he decided to head home without saying goodbye?

It wasn't something she would have expected from him, but mayhap he'd overheard *Mammi* Ruth complaining. Even if one didn't understand the Pennsylvania Dutch language, her ire was difficult to miss.

She poured water from the pitcher into the sink to begin washing dishes, but stopped when she saw the open barn door. Frowning, she peered closer, her heart lodging in her throat when she saw the bottom of a booted foot poking out through the opening.

David? Or someone else?

Elizabeth quickly dried her hands on a towel and reached for her cloak. She didn't hesitate to go outside, heading straight for the barn she'd avoided the day before.

Hurrying forward, she kept her gaze on the boot. She silently prayed whoever was sprawled there wasn't dead as she crossed the yard. When she grew closer, she heard a low groan and the boot moved a few inches.

"David?" she called loudly. "Is that you? Are you hurt?"

Another low groan, then the boot vanished from her line of sight. She quickened her pace, arriving at the doorway as David pulled himself upright, leaning heavily against the barn.

"What happened?" She instinctively put her arm around his waist to help support him.

"Someone was in here," he said. "He hit me on the head. Go, quickly. You must seek refuge in the house."

"Not without you." She wasn't leaving him here. Besides, there was no sign of the man who'd attacked him, likely the same person who'd shoved her the previous night. It made her angry, but there wasn't anything she could do about it now. "*Komm*, we will go together."

David didn't answer but managed two staggering steps forward. She tightened her grip around his waist, using all her strength to help him stay upright.

It took longer than it should have to cross the backyard to reach the house. There, he leaned against the building as she opened the door, then finally managed to cross the threshold.

"Over here, David." She steered him toward the sofa. He collapsed on the cushions, closing his eyes as if he'd used every ounce of his strength to get there.

And he probably had. She wanted to pepper him with questions about the attack, but his pale face and brackets of pain around his mouth prevented her from speaking. She reached over to lightly feel his head for a wound.

The egg-sized lump on the side of his head was upsetting. Who had done this? Jacob? It wasn't right for her to accuse a man without evidence, yet she couldn't imagine who else would so such a thing.

She hurried to the kitchen, dampened a cloth, then went outside to pack it with snow. It was the best she could do in the spur of the moment.

When she gently pressed the cloth against the knot on his temple, David opened his eyes.

"I'm fine," he said in a weak voice. He reached up to cover her hand with his. "No need to worry."

"Did you see the man who attacked you?" She gazed into his beautiful, clear blue eyes.

"No. It was too dark." He frowned and gently took the cold cloth from her hand to use it himself. "But tell me this, Elizabeth, why was he hiding inside your barn?"

"I don't know."

"You must know something," David said wryly. "I saw your footprints outside in the snow."

Of course he had. She should have known his keen gaze wouldn't miss a thing. She understood it was well past time to tell him what had happened, certain that he deserved the truth.

"Last evening, I thought I saw and heard someone along the side of the house. I went to investigate, following a set of fresh footprints to the barn. The door was open an inch, and I called out to whoever might be in there, but I did not get a response. I was too frightened to go inside, so I turned away. As I was walking back to the house someone came up behind me and shoved me down to the ground."

His eyes narrowed. "Someone pushed you? It wasn't a slip and fall? You were attacked?"

"*Ja.*" She shook her head, feeling guilty. "*Ach*, I'm terribly sorry. I should have told you the truth. I never expected you would be hurt as well."

"Jacob?" David asked.

She hesitated, then shrugged. "How can I say for certain sure? It's true I don't care for him, but why would he try to hurt me? Especially if he desires a courtship?"

"I don't know, but he certainly has a good reason to attack me," David said slowly. "After the way I helped you escape riding home with him, he may see me as some sort of rival."

She silently agreed with his assessment.

"Maybe he didn't really intend to hurt you," David continued. "He only shoved you down to the ground because he didn't want to get caught sneaking around your property."

"Mayhap you are right," she agreed. "Not that his actions make any sense. Certain sure he has better things to do. He has a large farm of his own, and caring for his livestock must keep him busy."

"Not busy enough," David muttered darkly.

"I don't like it, Elizabeth. You need to call the police."

"You know that is not our way," she chided.

"Then what?" David removed the cold wash-cloth from his temple. "What if you get hurt again?"

She took the cloth and carried it to the kitchen. Then she returned to sit beside him. "I shall bring my concerns to Bishop Bachman."

"Will the bishop confront Jacob?" he asked, pinning her with a stern look.

She hesitated. Would Bishop Bachman believe her about the intruder being Jacob? Mayhap not without proof. "I don't know, but he will alert the elders, which is enough, *ja*?"

"It's not enough for me." David sighed, then closed his eyes again. His drawn features concerned her. She sensed he was in far more pain than he was admitting to. "I should go," he murmured.

He should, but she knew that was impossible. "*Ach*, you can't walk all the way home in your condition. You'll never make it." If she had a horse and buggy, she would have offered to drive him. But she had not kept them, preferring to walk back and forth to the shop. Caring for *Mammi* Ruth and quilting while also caring for the livestock had proven to be too much for her to handle alone. "You must stay here and rest."

His eyes popped open. "No. Your mother-in-law would be terribly upset to find me here in the morning."

Mammi Ruth would have much to say on the subject; of that Elizabeth was certain. But it didn't matter. She would not allow David to walk all the way home in the winter with a head injury. "*Mammi* Ruth will get over it. It is our duty to care for those who are injured, *ja*? Your health is most important." She rose to her feet. "I'll fetch a pillow and blanket."

"One of your quilts?" The hopeful expression in his eyes made her smile.

"*Ach*, certain sure I have many to choose from." It didn't take long to go up to the second floor to find an extra pillow and quilt. When she returned to the living room, she inwardly winced as she realized she'd brought down one of her wedding quilts.

Thankfully, David didn't seem to notice. She could tell his head ached terribly, as he offered a wry smile, stretching out on the sofa. "Good night, Elizabeth."

"Good night." She had to force herself to turn and walk away.

As she washed her face and prepared for

bed, she secretly acknowledged that she liked the idea of David staying downstairs on her sofa, far too much.

David slept deeply for the first time in what seemed like forever. No nightmares of his past mistakes or of his recent run-in with the gunman had troubled him.

And when he'd awoken, the scent of cinnamon had told him he was in Elizabeth's house. Despite the irritable throbbing in his head, he smiled.

Then frowned. He should leave before Elizabeth and *Mammi* Ruth arose. It was the least he could do, sparing Elizabeth from another slew of complaints after she'd been so kind.

Moving gingerly, he sat up, then slowly stood. The room didn't undulate around him, which he took as a good sign. There was a chill in the air, so he added more wood to the stove.

Before he'd finished, he heard footsteps behind him. Turning, he smiled when he saw Elizabeth coming down the stairs. She was beautiful to his eyes, even with her blond hair tucked into her modest *kapp*. He appreciated her ivory skin and warm brown eyes.

"*Ach*, you're up early, David."

"So are you." He tucked his hands in his pockets. "I'm glad I could see you before I go."

"No need to rush off. You must stay for breakfast." She waved a hand toward the staircase behind her. "*Mammi* Ruth has asked for a tray to be brought to her room. She's not feeling well this morning."

The news was a welcome relief. He felt himself grinning like a little kid turned loose in the candy store with five bucks in hand. "In that case, I would like to stay for breakfast, thank you."

Elizabeth's blush deepened, and she hurried into the kitchen. He took a moment to use the facilities, then joined her.

"Coffee is ready." She gestured to the pot warming on the top of the stove.

He poured himself a mug and took a seat at the table, partially to stay out of her way, but mostly because he enjoyed watching her work. "I'd like to check out the barn after we eat."

"What?" She turned from the skillet to face him. "Why go back in there?"

He eyed her over the rim of his coffee. "Have you considered there may be a reason someone has chosen to hide inside?"

She frowned, then turned back to making eggs. "There is nothing there to find, if that's what you're thinking. After Adam's death, Jacob and the bishop took the livestock to other farmers. In return I am provided fresh eggs, meat and other vegetables and canned goods." She sighed and added, "Along with rides to and from the Amish Shoppe on inclement weather days."

He lowered his mug. "You haven't been inside the barn since his death?"

"That is correct." She didn't elaborate further.

David would have thought she'd avoided the barn because the memory of losing her husband would be too painful, except that she'd already told him that she wasn't mourning Adam, as theirs had been an arranged marriage.

Was it possible Jacob had hidden something inside? Maybe because he'd known she didn't use the barn for housing livestock?

But what? And why? If the man had a farm of his own, he wouldn't need to hide something here. It didn't make any sense.

Elizabeth put together a small tray for *Mammi* Ruth, then excused herself to take it upstairs. He rose and walked over to the sink, staring for long moments at the barn.

The situation bothered him. The Amish

community may take care of their own, but he knew Elizabeth and her mother-in-law were vulnerable here, two women all alone.

He thought again of the gunman at the Amish Shoppe. He couldn't see how that incident was related to this. He truly believed Jacob was responsible for attacking him, and for pushing Elizabeth, maybe to scare her into taking his offer of courtship.

It was the only thing that made sense.

After Elizabeth returned and began making more eggs, he asked, "Do you have a padlock for the barn?"

She shook her head. "*Ach*, we normally don't lock our doors. Besides, there's no need to lock an empty space."

"I would disagree, since we've both been attacked by someone hiding inside," he pointed out dryly. "I have a lock in my workshop we can use. I'll bring it here when I escort you home this evening."

"*Denke,*" she murmured. Soon the eggs were ready and she set two plates on the table.

He reached over to take her hand, feeling bold without *Mammi* Ruth there to glare at him. "I'd like to say grace."

Elizabeth's smile warmed his heart.

"Dear Lord, we ask You to bless this food,

bless this house, and provide healing to *Mammi* Ruth. We seek Your wisdom as we seek justice for those who intend us harm. Amen."

"Amen," Elizabeth echoed. Their fingers clung for a moment before she withdrew her hand. "That was a beautiful prayer, David."

"Not as beautiful as you." The moment the words left his mouth, he wished to take them back.

Elizabeth stiffened in her seat. "David, please don't misunderstand..."

"I don't," he quickly interjected, attempting to reassure her. "Please forgive me. I spoke without thinking."

She was silent for a moment, then said softly, "I value our friendship, David."

"As I do." He mentally kicked himself for upsetting her. "Maybe my brains are as scrambled as these eggs, which are delicious."

She frowned. "Shall I provide another cold cloth for your injury?"

"No need, I'm fine." He didn't want to admit how he'd suffered far worse during his stint in jail. The new guy always took a beating, or so he'd been told after waking up in the sick bay. Only that time, his entire body had been pummeled, not just his head. But that was then. He was a different man now. "What chores need tending before we leave?"

"Nothing for you. I will make sure *Mammi* Ruth is comfortable, then plan something for dinner before I go."

"I'll wash dishes."

She looked startled by this. "Men don't wash dishes."

He arched a brow. "This one does. I cook and clean for myself. Why not help you, too?"

Elizabeth looked perplexed by this but was prevented from saying anything when *Mammi* Ruth called from upstairs. The gist of her Pennsylvania Dutch, from what little he understood, was that she was finished with her meal and desired Elizabeth's help.

He had to grin when Elizabeth finished her eggs and bread before rising to her feet. She would never treat her mother-in-law poorly, but he had to admire her spunk in standing up for herself. No reason to instantly jump to meet *Mammi* Ruth's demands.

Once he'd finished his meal, he began washing the dishes, eyeing the barn. After the dishes were done, he pulled on his coat and boots and headed outside.

In the daylight, the barn was hardly threatening. The weather warmed a bit, melting the snow and making a mess of the footprints.

Not that he expected Bishop Bachman to come to see them for himself. Liam would, because cops took investigating crimes seriously, but he felt certain the Amish would simply speak to those involved, expecting compliance.

He pushed the door open and walked inside. The interior smelled musty from lack of use, despite the door being left open.

There were damp spots on the wooden floor, evidence of snow melting off boots. He could see exactly where the attacker must have stood when he'd grabbed David's jacket and pulled him inside.

Moving further into the barn, he found more scuff marks and damp spots throughout the interior. He frowned, realizing the intruder hadn't just hidden inside the barn, but had walked around.

He paused, raking his gaze over the structure. The barn wasn't as large as the one that had been turned into the Amish Shoppe, but it was rather spacious. A big-sized loft ran along the entire back side of the barn, and he imagined bales of hay had once been stored up there. The ladder looked sturdy, but he couldn't tell if anyone had climbed up the rungs recently.

If Jacob had been the one who'd hit him, why would he be hiding out in here? Not just one night, but two nights in a row?

He couldn't begin to fathom a motive for the man's strange behavior.

Other than that he clearly wanted to claim Elizabeth as his own.

David's fingers curled into fists at the thought of Jacob intentionally causing Elizabeth harm. Not to mention hitting him on the head, knocking him unconscious.

He walked the entire interior of the barn, but didn't find anything out of the ordinary. Which only reinforced his original thought.

Jacob had purposefully set out to scare Elizabeth.

David returned to the house, more determined than ever to secure the barn with a padlock. He entered the living room, his gaze immediately drawn to Elizabeth. She wore an apron over her light blue Amish dress, stirring something in a large pot on the stove.

"Smells great."

"*Ach*, 'tis only beef and vegetable soup." She glanced at him. "You spent a long time in the barn, *ja*?"

"Yes, it's obvious someone else has spent a lot of time in there, too." He hung his coat on the peg. "A sturdy padlock should take care of that problem."

She pursed her lips, then slowly nodded. "I agree."

He was glad she'd decided to go along with his plan. "Is there something else I can do for you?"

She shook her head. "I shall be ready to leave soon. Rest for now. Your head must still hurt, ain't so?"

"Not as badly as last night." He took off his boots and padded to the sofa. He took a moment to fold the quilt, setting it beneath the pillow.

Elizabeth finished preparing dinner, then went upstairs to check on *Mammi* Ruth, taking the quilt and pillow with her.

Soon they were bundled in their winter things and heading outside. Elizabeth closed the door behind her.

"I'm glad we're leaving early," she confided as they set out on foot. "Better this way, to avoid another confrontation with Jacob."

He glanced at her. "You really need to talk to Bishop Bachman about his persistence."

She grimaced and shrugged. "I will, but I believe Jacob will simply claim he is doing his role to support me in the wake of Adam's death. Many Amish elders have done the same, provided rides to and from the Amish Shoppe. He will claim his intent is no different."

"But they don't demand you go with them." He knew his anger toward Jacob came from a personal resentment of the man. "He doesn't seem to understand basic politeness."

"*Ja*, 'tis true," she agreed.

They walked for several moments in silence. David had promised himself to remain friendly with her, so he forced himself not to take her hand, the way he had last night.

Even though he badly wanted to.

A sharp retort shattered the silence. David reacted instinctively to the sound of gunfire. He yanked Elizabeth off the side of the road and toward some trees, quickly covering her with his body.

The same gunman who'd entered the Amish Shoppe last night? On the heels of that thought came a second shot.

A slice of bark flew from the tree just a few inches above his head. He ducked, dragging Elizabeth down to the ground with him.

This time, the shooter seemed intent on killing his target.

FOUR

Elizabeth swallowed a cry as the shot echoed around them. Crouched as they were behind two trees, she couldn't see the source of the gunfire. David's swift reaction had saved them, but for how long?

What was happening? Remembering how David had been fired upon at the Amish Shoppe, she was sure this was no accident. Not the handiwork of a novice hunter with poor aim.

Quite the opposite. His aim was far too good, as he'd nearly hit them both. If David hadn't been there, would she have survived this attack? Mayhap not. Grateful, she lifted her heart in prayer.

Lord, thank You for sending David to keep me safe. Please, continue to hold us in Your loving arms.

"Stay down," David whispered. She was

tempted to smile. In truth, moving was impossible with the way he had her sheltered against the tree, his body covering hers.

Then her heart sank as she realized they may be stuck there in the cold December wind, indefinitely. She shivered and tried to grab the edges of her cloak closer to her neck.

David didn't move for long moments. She appreciated his protection, but didn't want anything to happen to him, either. She peered out at their surroundings, trying to remember where the closest shelter might be.

The gunfire had stopped, but that didn't mean the hunter wasn't still out there, patiently waiting for them to reveal themselves.

The road they'd walked was to their left, but a wide expanse of snow-covered fields stretched beyond the wooded area to their right. In the distance, she could see Jacob Strauss's barn. Jacob's property was adjacent to hers, no doubt another reason he'd decided to court her.

Elizabeth tensed when she heard a whinny along with the clip-clop of a horse's hooves hitting the pavement.

"Jacob is coming," David whispered. "I'd like you to ride with him to the Amish Shoppe."

"What about you?" She frowned up at him. "Certain sure Jacob will take us both."

"I'm going to stay here and search for the shooter."

"No! Please, don't." She twisted so that she could see his face more clearly. "You were injured last night—'tis not smart for you to be running about in the cold."

"Instead, I should accept a ride from the man who likely assaulted me in the first place?" His tone was wry and held a note of steel.

"*Ach*, David, I understand your position. But we would be safe enough if we stay together, *ja*?" She hesitated, then added, "Please. I would rather stay with you than go alone with Jacob."

There was a long moment before he blew out a frustrated breath. "Okay, we'll stick together."

"*Denke*," she whispered.

When the horse and buggy came into view, David moved away from her just a few inches and raised his hand to attract Jacob's attention.

"Whoa," Jacob said, pulling at the reins. Then he scowled at them. "What is this? Why are you here?" Jacob looked from David to her, as if they'd been involved in something improper. She wanted to explain that David had saved her life, but David spoke first.

"Someone fired a gun at us." David's tone was curt. "We took cover near the tree, hoping the shooter would show himself. I would ask on Elizabeth's behalf that you might give us a ride to the Amish Shoppe. I would like to prevent her from being hurt."

Jacob appeared surprised, but then gave a brief nod. "I heard the gunfire," he admitted with a frown. "I thought mayhap a hunter had gotten turned around to have ended up this close to the road and to my property. And Elizabeth's, too," he hastily added.

"That was no hunter," David said firmly. The way he stared up at him, she felt he was waiting for Jacob to admit to assaulting him. But of course, Jacob didn't say anything about that. "Will you please consider giving us a ride?" David pressed.

Jacob nodded again, stood and offered his hand. Elizabeth forced herself to take it, allowing Jacob to help her into the buggy. David quickly vaulted up under his own power to join them.

She was squished between the two men, which provided some additional warmth. Yet being this close to them made her very aware of how she preferred David's unique scent, a mixture of her soap from when he'd washed up that morning, along with the hint of sawdust that clung to his skin.

She was aware that she was being ridiculous to think of such things. David was a dear friend, nothing more. And she was grateful to have his friendship. His companionship.

She slanted a look up at Jacob's stern profile. Was he truly capable of shoving her to the ground and striking David in the head?

If so, he was doing an excellent job of hiding his guilt.

"Is there a reason someone would shoot at you?" Jacob asked, leaning forward to look at David.

"No reason that I can think of for anyone to target me or to come after Elizabeth." David returned Jacob's stare. "Unless you can think of someone who might do that?"

"No, yet it appears walking back and forth each day isn't smart." Jacob turned his gaze on her. "I will drive you back and forth to work, starting tonight."

She wanted to decline his offer, but glanced at David to see what he thought. A pained expression crossed his face, before he slowly nodded. "Might be for the best, Elizabeth."

"Of course, it is for the best." Jacob was using his bossy, authoritative tone again, the one that put her teeth on edge.

"I will decide what is best for me." She wasn't in the mood to agree with spending another moment with Jacob.

Jacob appeared taken aback by her statement, but didn't say anything more as the large red barn of the Amish Shoppe came into view. They were not late, thanks to Jacob's buggy ride, but she was anxious to get inside.

Jacob pulled up in front of the front door, then jumped out to help her down. She accepted his hand, stepping back to give David room to come down.

"*Denke*, Jacob. I believe I will spend some time with my cousin Liam later today and as such, I will not require a ride home." She turned away to hurry inside, with David following right behind her.

Thankfully, Jacob didn't try to strong-arm her into changing her mind. Glancing back over her shoulder, she saw him jump into the buggy and turn back toward his farm.

One problem solved for the moment.

"Are you really going to talk to Liam?" David asked as he escorted her down the center aisle to their respective shops. "I plan to tell him about the gunfire, so there's no reason for you to be involved if you'd rather not."

She grimaced. "It's not our way to involve law enforcement in the Amish community, but I am concerned for you, David. Mayhap that was the same man who broke in here the other night." She hesitated, then added, "Liam should be told about what happened this morning."

"Aren't you worried Jacob will say something to the elders?" David's concern on her behalf was heartwarming. "I don't wish for you to suffer repercussions from the community."

"I will be fine, *ja*? There's nothing for you to worry about." She managed a smile as they reached their doors. "I would ask you to call Liam. When he arrives, we shall both speak to him about the gunfire nearly striking us this morning."

"And we'll also tell him about the person hiding in your barn, right?" David held her gaze.

The two assaults from someone hiding in her barn should be reported to the police. Especially if they were somehow linked together. But she shook her head. Mayhap it was a blurred line in the sand, but she felt certain sure Jacob had been the one in her barn.

But he couldn't have been the one who fired the gun at them. There hadn't been enough time for him to get the horse and buggy from his barn to reach them if he had done so.

"Not yet." She used her key to unlock the door to her quilt shop. "See you later, *ja*?"

"Yes, of course. I'm here if you need me." David slowly turned away to open his showroom.

She stood for a moment, feeling torn between David's *Englisch* world, and her Amish community. It was something that had never happened before.

Two months ago, when David had been kidnapped by bad men who'd used him to draw his niece Shauna out of hiding, she'd gone to the police to voice her concern. That seemed the right thing to do, as David was of the *Englisch* world.

But this morning's incident had taken place while they were still within the Amish community. She wanted to be true to her family, to her roots, to her traditions.

After removing her cloak, she sank into her sewing chair and bowed her head, seeking God's help and guidance in doing the right thing.

Whatever that might be.

* * *

When he opened his showroom, David tried not to let his frustration with Elizabeth bother him. He idly rubbed the sore spot on his scalp, a reminder of how blessed he was to have survived both the assault and the recent gunfire.

Customers wouldn't be arriving for twenty minutes yet, so he used that time to find the cell phone and call Liam directly, rather than going through the dispatcher.

"David? Are you okay?"

He couldn't help but smile at the alarm in Liam's voice. The sheriff knew David wouldn't call without a good reason. "Yes, but there was another incident this morning while Elizabeth and I were walking from her house to the Amish Shoppe. Someone fired two shots at us, Liam. It was only through God's grace that we escaped unscathed."

"I'll be right over," Liam said. "I'll need you to show me where you were when this happened."

"I can't leave until after closing. Friday and Saturday are our busiest days, especially considering Christmas is soon approaching." And he needed whatever income he could earn these next three days. After that, sales would be nonexistent.

"What if I bring Shauna to watch the show-room? It's important I find any evidence before the gunman attempts to get rid of it."

David sighed. "That's fine if Shauna doesn't mind helping." Shauna had worked his show-room before, so he had no qualms about her ability to sell his goods. In fact, she had helped him several times in the past. "But I'd still like to be back to work as quickly as possible. The Christmas rush is upon us, and I'd like to take advantage of that."

"Understood. We'll be there soon."

David disconnected from the call, then re-placed the phone. He tried to ignore the flash of guilt over using the phone for nonbusiness reasons.

Then again, if something happened to him, there wouldn't be a business. And the same logic applied to Elizabeth, too.

He glanced through the main showroom window to where Elizabeth was working on a quilt. Like him, she used the downtime over the winter months to build up her stock.

She was so pretty it wasn't easy to tear his gaze away. He quickly moved into the back workroom to examine the damaged baby cra-dle. The bullet had gone too far in for him to simply sand the damage away, so he set about measuring and making another panel to replace the damaged one.

He'd barely started hand sawing the board when he heard Shauna. "Uncle Davy? We're here."

After dusting off his hands, he went into the main showroom to join them. "Good to see you, Shauna."

"Liam told me about the two incidents of gunfire." His niece's blue eyes, mirror images of his own, were clouded with concern. "I don't like this. You need to stay with me and Liam for a while."

"And leave Elizabeth vulnerable? No." He hesitated, realizing that he and Elizabeth hadn't really discussed their next steps after the shops were closed for the day. Would she allow him to continue sleeping on her sofa? *Mammi* Ruth would not be supportive of that, but someone had been lurking in her barn.

And they'd been shot at.

What was next?

"David, do you have any idea who could be doing this?" Liam pinned him with a knowing gaze. "I feel like there's more to the story than you're telling me."

"I have some thoughts, but we can talk along the way to the area where the shooting took place." He glanced at Shauna. "Thank you for taking care of the customers for me."

"Any time," Shauna assured him.

He followed Liam through the shops to the main entrance. Thankfully, Liam had driven his personal SUV, rather than one of the police vehicles. As Elizabeth's cousin, Liam knew the Amish rarely came to law enforcement with their concerns.

As Liam drove, David quickly explained about the assault on Elizabeth, along with the one on him from someone hiding in Elizabeth's barn. "She won't be happy I'm telling you about the two assaults," David said. "You know the Amish prefer to handle their own issues. But she does want you to know about the gunfire, and I can't say for sure they aren't related."

"What happened after you were assaulted?" Liam asked.

He felt himself flush. "Elizabeth insisted I sleep on her sofa, which was very kind of her. However, I don't believe she'll allow me to do that again. I would hate to cause harm to her reputation, but her safety is a much bigger concern."

"Exactly. I'll talk to her, too and convince her to have you stay at least for a few days,"

Liam said. "I'd feel better if she wasn't alone in the house with Ruth."

"Ruth does not have a high opinion of me," David admitted. "But I won't allow her disdain to get in the way of keeping Elizabeth safe."

"I have a feeling Elizabeth's mother-in-law isn't happy in general," Liam said. "Elizabeth believes she's grieving over the loss of her son, which I can understand."

"Yes." David knew Liam had lost his wife and son a little over two years ago, but had found love again with Shauna. He was very happy for them.

Yet David privately thought that losing her son wasn't an excuse for *Mammi* Ruth to make everyone around her miserable, too. Liam had withdrawn after his tragedy but hadn't been angry with those around him. He sensed *Mammi* Ruth was angry that her son was gone while Elizabeth was still here.

"Slow down, Liam. The spot where we took cover is just a few yards ahead."

"Those trees?" Liam asked gesturing to the right.

"Yes."

Liam pulled over to the side of the road. He got out of the car, and David quickly joined him.

"We were here when the gunfire first rang

out." David stood in the spot they'd been less than an hour ago. "I pulled Elizabeth toward the trees, protecting her with my body, when we heard the second shot. I'm sure the bullet hit the tree inches from my head."

There was a long moment as Liam examined the tree. "Found it." Using a penknife, Liam pried the bullet free and dropped it into an evidence bag. "This slug is mangled worse than the one I pulled out of your baby cradle, but the lab may be able to match them up."

"That would be helpful." David gestured to the bullet. "Although if the shooter from this morning is the same one that broke into the Amish Shoppe the other night, I have more questions than answers."

Liam nodded thoughtfully. "Yeah. If the motive for breaking in wasn't robbery, then what? Clearly the guy picked the lock to get access to the place. Was he looking for information?"

"What kind of information?" David looked at the bullet hole in the tree. "And if that's all he wanted why shoot at us again? It doesn't make any sense."

"And you're sure the man who you saw at the shop wasn't this Jacob Strauss guy?" Liam asked.

"Jacob is very tall, and the guy I saw wasn't.

However, that doesn't mean Jacob didn't hire someone to do his dirty work. Jacob conveniently showed up to offer us a ride this morning, too." The more he considered the recent events, the more convinced he was that Jacob was involved. "I still think he believes scaring Elizabeth will cause her to accept his courtship."

"She's not interested?" Liam asked.

"No, she has made it clear she has no interest in getting married again," David assured him. "What's really interesting is that she said she'd rather walk with me, than ride with him." When he saw Liam's eyebrows lever up in surprise, he quickly added, "Because we're friends, nothing more."

"If you say so."

"I do. I'll always honor her wishes." David glanced around the area. "Is that all? I'd like to get back."

"Just give me a minute to see where the guy may have been standing." Liam strode away from the tree, at an angle that took him across the road. David tried to be patient but didn't think finding the spot where the shooter had stood would be very helpful.

When Liam headed farther away, David considered walking back to the Amish Shoppe. It wasn't that he didn't trust Shauna to look after his showroom, but more so that he didn't like being so far from Elizabeth.

What if the shooter had watched him leave with Liam? The guy could right now be stalking Elizabeth, waiting for the perfect opportunity to strike.

Without even realizing it, he took several steps away from Liam's SUV, heading down the side of the road.

"I found something," Liam called.

"What?" David swung back to look at where Liam stood a good hundred yards away. He jogged over to meet him, praying Liam had found evidence that would implicate Jacob Strauss.

Or the man he'd paid to shoot at them.

Liam was kneeling on the ground near a scrubby bush. As David joined him, he could see a straight line from this location to the trees where they'd found the bullet.

"This must have fallen out of his pocket." Liam pointed at a scrap of paper dampened by the snow. "It's a partial business card, with a logo in the corner."

David dropped down to look at it more closely. The snow made the colors blur, but the green blotch didn't look familiar. "Why is this helpful?"

Liam stared for a moment, then snapped his fingers. "It looks a little like the logo for The Green Lake Grill Bar and Restaurant. Maybe the shooter spent some time there."

"It's possible." The Amish did not frequent English establishments, especially not a place that offered alcoholic beverages. And it didn't make sense that Jacob would meet there to hire someone to shoot at them, either. Wouldn't he try to find someone he knew within the Amish community?

A chill snaked down his spine. Was he wrong about Jacob? Was it possible there was another motive for these attacks?

Had his criminal past finally caught up with him?

FIVE

"Your quilts are so beautiful, Elizabeth," Shauna said with a smile. "I love the ones you've made for Christmas, with the red and green patterned squares. Oh, and thank you again for gifting me and Liam a wedding quilt. We love it."

"*Wilkom*, Shauna. It was my pleasure. You have made my cousin very happy, ain't so?"

"The feeling is mutual," Shauna assured her.

"David has not yet returned?" Elizabeth was far too aware of how long David and Liam had been gone. She missed him, which didn't make any sense as they each took care of their own shops. It wasn't as if she as accustomed to chatting with David all day.

They had gotten in the habit of sharing lunch together at the Sunshine Café. Would David return in time? Had he and Liam found something near the spot where someone had fired a gun at them?

She chided herself for being so curious. Normally Liam wouldn't be investigating an incident involving the Amish.

Yet she couldn't help feeling on edge. The niggling concern didn't go away until she saw David and Liam walking down the center aisle of the barn. Considering their grim expressions, she suspected the news was not good.

"Is everything okay?" She stepped forward to greet them. "*Ach*, you didn't run into trouble, did you?"

"Everything is fine," David assured her. He smiled, but the light didn't reach his blue eyes. "Liam found the bullet and will see if it matches the one embedded in the baby cradle."

"Elizabeth, are you familiar with the Green Lake Grill?" Liam asked.

"No, certain sure I have never been there. Why do you ask?"

"We've been there, Liam," Shauna said. "But just that one time. There were several rough-looking guys hanging out, so we decided against staying to eat."

"I remember," Liam said dryly. "But Elizabeth, I'm curious if you've heard of any Amish going there."

She shook her head, wondering what they were getting at. "No, Liam. I have never heard of the place, and it would be unusual for any-one within the Amish community to go there."

"I know it's not normal practice," Liam admitted. "But I have seen several Amish men around town. It wouldn't be completely unheard of for them to stop at a restaurant to eat."

"That much is true." She glanced between David and Liam. "Is there a connection to the Green Lake Grill, then?"

"No connection, yet." A wry smile creased her cousin's features. "You know it's my job to ask a lot of questions, without giving answers."

She narrowed her gaze. "It's not an admirable trait."

That made him chuckle. "Sorry, cousin, but my goal is to bring bad guys to justice, which means finding evidence that can be used to prove guilt."

To be fair, Liam was very good at his job. But among the Amish, justice and punishment were handled much differently. "That's your choice, Liam."

"Yes, it is." Liam glanced at Shauna. "I'm heading back. Do you want to stay here or come with me?"

Shauna looked torn. "David? Do you need my help?"

"No need to stay, Shauna. Go with Liam. I'll

be fine." Even as David spoke, a couple wandered into his shop. He moved over to greet them politely, but then stepped back to give them space to browse.

There was much to admire about David McKay. He was strong and gentle at the same time, and she liked the way he managed his furniture by displaying her quilts. She had to force herself to return to her store.

Before she could pick up the quilt she was working on, customers came in to view her stock, gravitating toward the Christmas display. From that point on, there was a steady stream of customers to keep her and David very busy.

A good busy. Tomorrow was Saturday, the last day of work for the week. After that, the shops would not be open again for business until the following Wednesday. And even then, only for two days before they'd close for the holiday.

Three days of not seeing or spending time with David. On the heels of that thought came a sense of shame. Elizabeth knew she was blessed beyond measure.

Wanting something that was out of reach was wrong.

Mayhap it was a good thing Sunday was

coming up soon. She certainly needed to attend church services.

As the hour passed noon, her stomach began to rumble with hunger. Yet the crowd of shoppers hadn't abated at all. If anything, there seemed to be even more of them.

When she'd finished ringing up another sale of a Christmas quilt, she saw David approach. He held two bags in his hands. "I've brought lunch."

"*Ach*, you didn't need to do that." She made it a habit to pay for her own meals.

"I wanted to." David handed her one of the bags. "I'd like to stay, but there isn't time. If I'd known it would be this busy, I'd have asked Shauna to stay and help."

"*Sehr gut* to be busy, though, *ja*?" She gratefully accepted the meal. "Once Christmas has passed, the crowds will diminish. *Denke* for lunch, David."

"You haven't seen Jacob, have you?" David asked.

She shook her head. "No, he wouldn't come here. He has his farm to care for."

"Okay." David offered a quick smile, then turned away to walk back to his store.

As she took a quick bite of the sandwich David had brought her, she wondered why he'd asked about Jacob. But the steady stream of customers didn't provide idle time to think.

The crowd finally thinned out thirty minutes before closing. She quickly straightened the various displays, then placed her current quilt pieces together in a bag to take back home with her.

When she'd finished, David joined her. "Elizabeth, I've arranged for Liam to drive you home."

"You did?" She had secretly looked forward to the walk home with David.

"It's for your safety, Elizabeth." His gaze was serious. "We don't know who shoved you to the ground or fired those shots at us."

She knew accepting Liam's help was the right thing to do. "*Ach*, that's fine. I appreciate the ride. *Denke*."

"There's one more thing." David grimaced and avoided her direct gaze. "I would like to sleep on your sofa again. Only to protect you and *Mammi* Ruth," he hastened to assure her. "Please know I would never risk ruining our friendship by doing anything improper. But I worry about the two of you being in the house alone."

"I see." She ducked her head as she wrestled with his request. It wasn't that she didn't trust him. But having him stay would cause a stir in the Amish community. Even with *Mammi* Ruth as a chaperone, there were many who would look down upon her.

Then again, her closest neighbor was Jacob and she would much rather have David sleeping on her sofa than go to him for help. Mayhap that was exactly what Jacob wanted—for her to seek shelter with him.

"I accept your kind offer, David." She mustered a smile. "I would appreciate you staying for a few days."

"You would?" He looked pleasantly surprised. "Oh, thank you, Elizabeth. I was trying to come up with a way to sleep in the barn without freezing to death."

"Don't even say such a thing! I wouldn't want you to do something that drastic."

"Your safety is what is most important," David told her. "So, then, when Liam arrives I hope you won't mind stopping at my house so I can pick up a few personal things."

"That's fine." His comment made her realize this was the reason he'd asked Liam to drive her home. Yet she could understand his wanting a change of clothes and perhaps a razor. As an unmarried man, he shaved his beard each day the way the Amish men did. Only married men wore beards, yet she secretly preferred David's face as it was.

Not that his choice to shave or not was hers to make. Still, the way he honored Amish traditions made her smile.

"Are you ready?" David asked. "I told Liam we would meet him out front. That way, if Jacob is there, he'll see us leaving with the sheriff."

The comment gave her pause. "Did you tell Liam about Jacob's attempt to court me?"

There was a slight hesitation before he inclined his head. "Yes, but only because Liam needs the big picture. You must realize Jacob is still a suspect."

A stab of disappointment hit hard. She'd expected David to keep the investigation centered on the gunfire, not on the other events.

"Don't be angry," David said softly. "I only want you to be safe."

"Without taking into concern what I want?"

He didn't answer. Elizabeth turned away to don her cloak. As upset as she was, she wasn't ready to refuse David's offer to sleep on the sofa.

She told herself that *Mammi* Ruth needed to be safe, too.

But deep down, she knew the truth was that she cared about David.

More than she should.

* * *

He didn't like making Elizabeth angry, but he wasn't sorry that he'd told Liam about the series of events that had taken place over the past twenty-four hours.

As they walked through the now empty Amish Shoppe, he glanced at her. "There's something more you need to know."

"There is?" Apprehension darkened her eyes.

"About me, my past." David's chest tightened. She could very well refuse to let him stay once she knew the truth. Yet he didn't want to lie.

In fact, this conversation was something he should have had months ago.

"I'm a former criminal, Elizabeth. I did four years in prison for manslaughter."

She abruptly stopped and turned to face him. "You did?"

"Yes." He cleared his throat. "I could tell you that my intentions were honorable, that I was only looking out for a woman who was being harassed by a man who touched her inappropriately, but that is mostly an excuse. The truth is, I let my anger get the best of me. And while he struck me first, we exchanged blows. After the third time he came at me, I hit him hard enough that he stumbled backward, striking his head against the edge of a table. The blow was severe enough to kill him."

Her jaw dropped, but then she reached for his hand. "That must have been terrible."

"It was." He could barely look at her. "I have turned my life around since then. I've found God and am working hard to earn God's forgiveness, but you need to know the truth about me."

"*Ach*, David, I do know you. We are all sinners, ain't so?"

"Some worse than others," he murmured. "Anyway, I think it's possible that we have two different bad guys coming after us. Jacob could be trying to scare you into marrying him, and the shooter could be related to my past."

"After all this time?" she asked with a frown.

"The way Shauna and I had been kidnapped last October, probably made the news." He and Liam had discussed the possibility at length on the ride back to the Amish Shoppe. "The young man who died by my hand, Carson Wells, came from a well-to-do family. One with connections in politics. When I was finished with probation, I relocated to Green Lake from Madison. Carson's family may have seen the news and found me here."

"I see." She frowned. "I don't like the idea of

you being in danger. Is there something Liam can do about that?"

"He's going to look into it," David assured her. Then he forced himself to look into her eyes. "Does knowing what I've done change how you feel about me?"

"No, David, why should it?" She looked confused. "As I said we are all guilty of sin, and none of us are perfect. And I'm very glad you found God."

He was overwhelmed with relief. "I—thank you. I feared you would prefer not to be associated with me."

"David? Oh, there you are." Liam came inside to catch up with them. "Are you ready to go?"

"I think so, yes." He glanced at Elizabeth, who nodded.

"Great." Liam escorted them outside. David took a moment to lock the main doors, then heard a horse and buggy approaching.

Swallowing a groan, he turned to see Jacob riding toward them. The Amish man's persistence in seeking Elizabeth's courtship was wearing thin.

He felt Elizabeth stiffen beside him. But when Liam moved as if to approach, she hurried over to put a hand on her cousin's arm. "Please, allow me to talk to him, *ja*?"

Liam frowned. "I would like to ask him a few questions."

"No, Liam." She stood firm. "If you pursue this investigation into Jacob, I will accept Jacob's ride home and refuse to allow David to stay on my sofa. You know the Amish will not talk to you, anyway, and they will be insulted by your questions. There's no reason for you to interfere."

David wanted to protest, but managed to bite his tongue. Elizabeth walked over to the buggy. She was too far away for him to hear what she told Jacob, but the grim expression on the Amish's man's face indicated he was not happy.

After a long moment Jacob nodded and turned away. Elizabeth watched him leave for a few moments, then came back to join them. "I believe Jacob finally understands my position and has agreed to stop offering me rides to and from the Amish Shoppe unless requested."

"Good," David muttered, thinking that it was about time he got the message.

"*Komm*, we should go," Elizabeth said. "The temperature is dropping, ain't so?"

Liam looked annoyed, but opened the passenger door of his SUV for Elizabeth. David climbed into the back. "What did you say to him?"

She glanced over her shoulder. "I explained that his persistence was scaring me and asked if he had been hiding in my barn. He looked surprised by that, and of course denied doing such a thing. Then I explained how I planned to discuss his behavior with Bishop Bachman after church services on Sunday, unless he stopped coming by without invitation."

"And he agreed?" David asked.

"He did, especially since I told him that as my neighbor I would certain sure reach out if I needed help." Elizabeth shrugged and glanced at Liam. "Jacob denied being outside my house last night, or the night before. I'm satisfied that he is aware of my concerns. I suspect he will leave me alone."

For now, David thought grimly.

"I still would have liked to talk to him myself," Liam said with a sigh. "But I will respect your wishes."

"*Denke.*"

Liam shook his head as he started the car. He turned the SUV in the opposite direction from the way Jacob had gone. David's house was off a rural highway, roughly a mile and a half from the Amish Shoppe, but in the complete opposite direction of the Amish community.

The walk was refreshing, most of the time. But now he didn't like the way he was so far from Elizabeth.

"Have you changed your mind about me staying with you?" he asked. "I can ask Liam to simply drop me off at home, if you think my being there will cause trouble."

His heart sank when she hesitated. "It may be best if you stay away, David. I believe Jacob will leave me alone, now. There's no reason for you to sleep on the sofa, *ja*?"

He grimaced and repeated Liam's words. "I believe you may still be in danger, but I'll respect your decision."

No one spoke for several minutes as Liam navigated the slippery highway. He pulled into David's driveway and shifted the SUV into Park. "Do you want me to wait a minute?"

He hesitated, realizing it had been nearly four days since he'd been back, then shook his head. "I should be fine."

"*Ach*, just go in with him, Liam. Certain sure it will only take a few minutes."

David lightly touched Elizabeth's shoulder. "Good night. I will see you tomorrow."

"*Sehr gut*, David. Take care."

He wondered if the regret in her gaze was real or a figment of his imagination. He forced himself to push out of the SUV, slamming the door behind him.

Liam waited for him to round the vehicle. "I'm sorry Elizabeth changed her mind."

"Me, too." He glanced at Liam. "I still think Jacob is responsible, at least for pushing her and striking me. But it's possible Elizabeth's approach will cause him to hold back for a while. Especially since he knows she has the bishop's ear."

"You told her about doing jail time?" Liam asked.

He nodded and pushed open the front door. "Yes, and that may have contributed to her refusal to have me stay the night on her sofa."

"I don't think so," Liam protested. "She's not like that."

But David wasn't listening. He abruptly stopped and stared at the ransacked interior of his house.

"Stay back." Liam pushed him aside and pulled his weapon. "Go back out to the SUV while I take a look around."

"I'm not leaving you alone," David said grimly.

"You're not armed," Liam shot back. "I'm a cop. You're only going to be in my way."

David ignored him. This was his house, and therefore, his problem.

"Stay behind me, then," Liam muttered. He moved forward, checking the living area, the kitchen, then moving down the hallway to the bedrooms and the single bathroom.

Every room had been touched by the person who'd done this. To be fair, his handmade furniture had held up well. It was clear the intruder had taken a knife to several of the structures, but without causing much damage.

Maybe that was something he could use to market his furniture. *Durable enough to withstand acts of vandalism.*

Yeah, maybe not.

"I'll check the basement," Liam said, brushing past him.

David stood for a moment, his mind reeling. This could have happened any time in the past four days. Before he'd seen the intruder that night in the Amish Shoppe.

Had it been the same man? Or was Jacob responsible, viewing him as a threat to courting Elizabeth?

Anything was possible. Yet somehow, this ransacking of his personal space felt viciously personal.

"No one downstairs," Liam announced, returning to the main level. "Do you always leave your door unlocked?"

"Yes." He shrugged when Liam rolled his eyes. "It wouldn't have mattered. The person who did this would have broken the door down if it had been locked. Clearly there was no attempt to conceal the fact he was here."

"When were you here last?" Liam asked.

"Monday night. I worked all day Tuesday, then stayed the night so that I could be there when the shops opened Wednesday morning. Tomorrow is Saturday, so that's four days."

"And the intruder shot at you Wednesday night in the Amish Shoppe then again this morning?" Liam frowned. "I don't like it."

David didn't like it, either. And worse, he was concerned that he may have been followed to Elizabeth's house. If so, that changed things. She wouldn't like it, but he would insist on spending the night on her sofa.

He'd brought danger to her doorstep. The least he could do was to be there to protect her.

SIX

The grim expressions on both David and Liam's faces did not bode well. David had a duffel bag slung over his shoulder. Elizabeth assumed that meant he would be staying with Liam.

David stored the duffel in the back seat, before sliding in. "I'm afraid I have bad news. Someone ransacked my house."

She twisted in her seat to face him. "When did this happen?"

"I haven't been home in several days, so I can't say for sure." David's gaze locked on hers. "But I need to stay on your sofa, Elizabeth. It's possible the intruder followed me to your place, and waited for us to walk by this morning. If he knows where you live…" He shook his head. "I'm sorry, but I can't take that risk. Please don't ask me to stay away. I feel responsible for placing you in danger."

"*Ach*, this is not your fault, David." She couldn't believe the man who'd fired at them had been aiming at David, not her. Was it possible Jacob wasn't responsible? The news was sobering, but she also felt a hint of relief. She'd been determined to do the right thing by staying away from David, especially since Jacob had agreed to leave her alone, but there was no denying she'd feel safer with him nearby.

His presence would be a problem for *Mammi* Ruth, though. And she didn't relish listening to her mother-in-law's complaints.

"I would like you to let David stay, too," Liam said, breaking into her thoughts. "I stopped by the Green Lake Grill but haven't found anything helpful. Until I know more, I'd rather you both take extra safety precautions."

"I understand," she murmured.

"If you won't let David stay, the other alternative is to move you, Ruth and David to my place to stay with me and Shauna. It will be cramped, though—our house isn't that big."

She drew in a deep breath and let it out slowly. "*Ach*, no need for that, Liam. David is *wilkom* to stay with us. I will smooth things over with *Mammi* Ruth."

"I can help with the chores," David said.

"*Denke*, I know you will." She managed a

reassuring smile, deciding to trust in God's plan for her. "Let's get home, then, *ja*?"

"Thank you," David said, as if she were doing him a favor. When in truth it was the other way around.

His friendship was a blessing. Which was why she was determined to keep her attraction in check. Marriage didn't interest her, and even if she wanted to consider it, she had *Mammi* Ruth to care for.

The grieving mother deserved to be comfortable in her own home.

Less than fifteen minutes later, Liam pulled up in front of her house. The lantern in the upstairs bedroom was the only light visible, and Elizabeth felt a bit guilty for leaving the woman for so long.

"*Denke*, Liam." She moved to push open her door, but David was already there, opening it for her.

She hurried inside, with David following close behind. After removing her cloak and wiping the snow off her boots, she glanced at David. "I must see to *Mammi* Ruth."

"I'll stoke the fire."

Her mother-in-law was sitting in her chair, reading the Bible. "*Ach*, my apologies for the delay. How are you feeling?"

"Weak, but otherwise fine," she admitted.

Elizabeth privately thought she would be stronger if she moved around more, doing things for herself, but mayhap she wasn't being fair. "I have beef vegetable soup and bread for dinner. Would you like to come down to join us?"

"Us?" *Mammi* Ruth's eyes narrowed. "Did you invite that *Englischer* to stay for dinner again?"

"Yes." Elizabeth decided to confront the issue head-on. "David is a friend, and his home has been damaged. He needed a place to stay, and I offered him the chance to sleep on the sofa. Providing for those in need is what God expects of us, ain't so?"

Ruth scowled, glanced down at the Bible in her hands and said nothing.

"*Komm*, shall we get you downstairs for dinner? Certain sure it's best to move around a bit."

Her mother-in-law seemed indecisive. Elizabeth knew she didn't want to spend time with David, yet she probably also didn't want the two of them to be alone.

"*Mammi* Ruth, we are just friends, nothing more." Elizabeth rested her hand on the older woman's arm. "Please don't worry. I have no plans to marry again."

"Humph." *Mammi* Ruth didn't look convinced. "Help me up. I'll join you downstairs."

Elizabeth assisted the woman to her feet, and helped her don a fresh dress and apron. Ruth leaned against her, as if she was indeed weak.

Together they carefully navigated the stairs down to the first floor. David was busy at the stove, and the warmth radiating through the room brought a flush to her cheeks.

"It's nice to see you again, Mrs. Walton." David's tone was very respectful.

"You may call me *Mammi* Ruth," her mother-in-law said.

If David noticed she didn't return his greeting, he didn't let on.

Thanks to the prep work she'd done earlier that morning, which seemed like a lifetime ago after everything that had happened since then, the meal was soon ready.

David bowed his head and said grace. "Dear Lord, we thank You for providing this wonderful food we are about to enjoy. We also thank You for seeing us safely through another day, and we ask for Your continued blessings, amen."

"Amen," Elizabeth echoed. Then she repeated the blessing in Pennsylvania Dutch, for Ruth's sake.

"I guess I need to step up and learn the language," David murmured.

She smiled. "Don't worry, I am happy to translate. And many of the younger generation of Amish speak *Englisch*."

"But not the elders," David said. "I've picked up some of your native language from church services."

"You'll be attending services with us on Sunday?" *Mammi* Ruth asked.

"I would like to," David said. "If you will allow me."

"Certain sure you're welcome, David." Elizabeth glanced at Ruth, silently daring her to argue. "God's word is open to all who wish to hear, ain't so?"

"Ja," Ruth grudgingly admitted.

"Sehr gut." Elizabeth dug into her meal, suddenly famished. She had to smile when she saw how eagerly Ruth ate, too.

Throughout the meal, Elizabeth chatted about how many customers they saw at the Amish Shoppe, hoping to deflect any negative conversation about David's presence.

When they finished eating, she helped Ruth upstairs. By the time she'd returned to the kitchen, David had finished the dishes.

"I think that went well." His blue eyes gleamed. "She's beginning to like me."

"Mayhap that is true." Although Elizabeth wasn't entirely convinced. She glanced over to the sofa, his duffel bag on the floor beside it. "I'll get the pillow and quilt for you, *ja*? Is there anything else you need?"

"No, but I plan to look around outside before I retire for the night, so don't be surprised if you see me outside."

Her entire body went tense. "Are you sure that's a good idea?"

"I'm here to keep you and *Mammi* Ruth safe," he said gently. "I'll be fine."

Many Amish men had rifles to use for hunting, but she'd gotten rid of Adam's. Now she wished she'd kept it.

David donned his coat and hat, then headed outside. She quickly went up to get the pillow and quilt, then returned to watch his progress through the windows. She went as far as to move from one to the next to keep him in view.

When he returned unharmed, she let out a sigh. "Did you find anything?"

"All is well," he confirmed.

"Do you really think the gunfire is related to your past?" She felt nervous bringing up what was obviously a sore subject. "After all this time?"

"It is a possibility I cannot afford to ignore," David said. "I can't blame Carson Wells's family for being upset. His parents lost their son, and that is difficult to accept."

She wanted to reach out to offer some comfort, but stayed where she was. "You mentioned he started the fight. And that he was inappropriate with a woman, *ja*?"

"Yes." He grimaced. "But don't you see? I lost my temper. And losing control of my anger killed a man. It's something I've had to learn to live with for the past six years."

"I understand how difficult that must be. But don't judge yourself too harshly."

"I must take responsibility for my actions," he said firmly. "Good night, Elizabeth. I'll see you in the morning."

"Good night." She forced herself to head up to her room. While some might call her foolish, David's troubled past didn't bother her. She admired the man he was now, however that man came to be.

Oddly enough, she couldn't wipe the silly smile from her face.

Being in danger was never good, but for the

first time in months, she was looking forward to the next few days.

To spending more time with David.

By the time he'd finished walking Elizabeth's property, he'd convinced himself that he'd overreacted to the level of danger. The way she'd spoken to Jacob must have been enough to convince the man to let it go.

Yet even if Jacob had been behind the two incidents in Elizabeth's barn, there was still the gunfire to consider.

Not to mention, the ransacking of his house.

He was grateful that Elizabeth didn't seem to hold his criminal past against him. Maybe because they were friends, with no possibility of anything more.

Any woman would surely think twice about marrying a man who had killed someone.

He fed more wood into the fire, washed up in the bathroom, then took off his boots and stretched out on the sofa. Elizabeth's quilt was plenty warm, and the sofa more comfortable than the cot in his workroom, but sleep wouldn't come.

The memories of the worst night of his life were as clear as if they'd happened yesterday. Carson Wells had been so arrogant, a spoiled rich kid who was used to getting anything he wanted. The way he'd inappropriately touched Amanda, the waitress at the pub, had made the girl angry. She'd told him several times to stop grabbing her bottom, but Carson had only sneered at her. As if what she wanted didn't matter.

David's intentions had been honorable when he'd approached the young man. He'd politely but firmly told Carson to keep his hands to himself. But his words had the opposite effect. Carson had jumped to his feet, roughly telling David to mind his own business. Amanda hadn't been David's girlfriend, but that hadn't stopped him from facing off with Carson.

The kid threw the first punch, and out of nowhere a red haze of fury had clouded his vision. David had struck back, once, twice. Then when the kid came at him a third time, he put every ounce of his strength behind the blow that had sent the kid flying off his feet.

Unfortunately, Carson's head had struck the corner of the bar at just the right angle to do irreversible damage. The kid was dead by the time he'd hit the ground.

Carson's wealthy family carried a lot of clout in Madison, Wisconsin. His parents were large supporters of the governor, and the Madison

district attorney had wasted no time in arresting David for second-degree murder.

David hadn't been able to afford an attorney,
so he'd been assigned a public defender. Nice
enough guy who'd convinced David to accept
a plea deal of manslaughter. The only witness
who'd agreed to testify on his behalf had been
Amanda herself, but no one else dared to go
up against the Wells family by corroborating
his story about how Carson had thrown the
first punch. And even then, striking first didn't
mean the kid had deserved to die.

He squeezed his eyes shut, trying to erase
the image.

Was Jacob responsible for the wreckage in
his house? Or was someone seeking revenge
for what happened to Carson Wells?

Both were strong possibilities.

Maybe this was God's way of letting him
know he should sell the place. It was something he'd considered since he and Shauna had
been kidnapped by gunpoint and held against
their will. Yet his land, including his modest
ranch home, was one of the few assets he had
to offer if he ever found a woman to share his
life with.

A future that was far out of reach, since
the only woman he was remotely interested

in wanted nothing to do with marriage and family.

He finally fell into a restless slumber. But he woke often, the slightest noise sending him bolt upright on the sofa.

Around four thirty in the morning he gave up trying to sleep. Hard work was the best antidote for being on edge. After feeding more wood into the stove, he pulled on his boots and headed outside.

The darkness enveloped him, but he wasn't afraid. The snow made it easy to see if anyone was nearby and there were no additional footprints indicating an intruder had been there.

He went to the woodpile, eyeing the long tree branches lying nearby. No one had touched them since he'd been there the night before. He wondered why Jacob hadn't taken care of the chore for Elizabeth. It would have been smarter of him to do that than badger the woman about accepting a ride in his buggy to and from the Amish Shoppe.

David lifted the ax, resting it on his shoulder. For a moment he hesitated, fearing the sound would carry inside and wake the women. Then he went to work.

Chopping wood was oddly soothing. He quickly fell into an easy rhythm, the woodpile growing from his efforts. He finally took a break, only to hear Elizabeth calling to him.

"David? We shall break our fast soon, *ja*?"

He turned to see her standing in the doorway, a shawl clutched around her shoulders. Her beauty, as always, took his breath away.

"Coming." He waved, then bent to grab several logs to take inside. When he stood, a flash of something reddish orange caught the corner his eye.

He turned with a frown, staring at the odd glow coming from somewhere off in the distance. Too far away to see what it was, yet still visible thanks to the early morning darkness at this time of the year.

From what he could tell, the glow was in the opposite direction than the rest of the Amish community.

Christmas decorations of some sort?

Then he realized it was likely a fire. Maybe the result of a very dry Christmas tree igniting from an old string of lights. If he had a phone, he'd call 911 to let someone know, but he'd left it at the Amish Shoppe.

Hopefully, someone else would see it and make the call. He turned to walk back to the house.

"*Denke*, David. You've provided more than

enough wood for us. But you didn't have to start working so early in the morning. The shops don't open for a while, yet. We have plenty of time."

"I was awake anyway." There was no reason to bother her with his inability to sleep. "And happy to do the work."

Elizabeth smiled. "*Mammi* Ruth wishes to break her fast while staying in her room this morning. Give me a few minutes to take this tray up, then we can sit down to eat."

"That sounds wonderful." When she left, he hurried over to use the facilities, relieved to have time to wash up before it was time to eat. The physical labor of chopping wood had invigorated him, his earlier troubles seeming to have disappeared.

He was looking forward to what would likely be the busiest day of the season.

Elizabeth returned to the kitchen. After filling their plates, she sat down beside him. Then she surprised him by taking his hand in hers.

"Gracious Lord, we thank You for this wonderful meal. We ask that You continue to keep us safe in Your loving care, amen."

"Amen." He stared at their joined hands for a moment before meeting her gaze. "That was nice."

"Certain sure." She released his hand and began to eat. Was it his imagination or was she blushing?

He didn't want to make her feel uncomfortable, so he tried to concentrate on what needed to be accomplished later that day. He doubted there would be time to finish the baby cradle, but thankfully, he had already finished the quilt rack display he'd made for Elizabeth.

The Amish didn't routinely exchange large gifts for Christmas, but he'd hoped that she would accept this one from him.

Thankfully, he hadn't left it at his house, where the intruder may have damaged it. It was safely hidden in his workshop.

He was so lost in his thoughts that he didn't hear the car engine approaching outside.

"David? I believe someone is here."

Taking one last bite of his toast, he stood and moved toward the door. He highly doubted that the gunman would simply drive up to confront them, but he opened the door cautiously, peering out to see who was there.

Recognizing Liam's SUV, he pushed the door open and stepped outside. "Liam? What brings you here?"

"I'm afraid I have bad news." Liam gestured

for him to come closer. He did so, closing the door behind him.

"Bad news related to the gunman?" A grim expression was etched on Liam's face. "Do you know who he is?"

"No, but I know what he's done." Liam stepped closer, lightly grasping his arm. "There was a fire, David."

Remembering the reddish orange glow in the distance he nodded. "I thought I saw it, earlier. I would have called, but I didn't bring the mobile phone to Elizabeth's."

Liam looked at him oddly. "It was your house."

Shock rippled through him. "My house?"

"Yes. And I'm afraid that by the time the call came in, the blaze was out of control. There's nothing left, David. Your house is a total loss."

A total loss. The words reverberated through his mind as he grappled with the news. Gone. His house was gone.

Not by accident, either. He knew without being told the fire had been set on purpose.

SEVEN

Elizabeth had come outside in time to hear Liam's shocking news. David's home was gone, destroyed by a fire. She, too, had seen the odd orange glow in the distance, but had never considered the source to be David's home.

"What happened, Liam?" She pulled her shawl tighter around her shoulders as she stepped closer. "How did the fire start?"

"The firefighters haven't said for sure, but they believe it was set on purpose. There's no obvious evidence like gas cans or anything left behind, but one of them thought they could smell an accelerant." Liam turned to face David. "I'm glad you were here with Elizabeth last night, or the outcome of this terrible event may have been much worse."

She shivered at what Liam had implied. To think David may have been lost forever if she hadn't allowed him to come sleep on her sofa was inconceivable.

There was much to be thankful for, certainly. She was glad now that she hadn't let *Mammi* Ruth prevent her from allowing David to stay.

"Will you take me there?" David asked.

She looked up with a frown. "We'll both go. We can stop on the way to the Amish Shoppe, *ja*?"

"I don't know," Liam started, but David quickly interjected.

"Please, Liam. We need a ride at the very least. Can you wait here for a few minutes? It's best if I don't leave Elizabeth here alone. We need to stick together."

"I understand, but you should know there isn't much to see, just ashes and piles of charred wood." Liam hesitated, then added, "You should call your insurance company very soon, although they may not be open on Saturday."

David glanced at her, then shrugged. "No need, I let my policy lapse."

"What? Why did you do that?" Liam looked shocked but Elizabeth understood. The Amish didn't buy insurance. They simply supported each other in rebuilding.

Yet the Amish community wouldn't band together to rebuild David's home as he was still considered an outsider.

"I built the ranch house myself the first time," David said calmly. "I can rebuild it again if I so choose."

"But the cost of materials, the appliances, such as there were..." Liam shook his head. "I don't think you should have let the policy lapse. But of course you're welcome to stay with us. Shauna will insist."

"I appreciate that," David said. "But don't forget I can easily live in my workroom, too. I stayed there more often than not over these past few months." He managed a weak smile. "I'll be fine."

"*Ach*, David, you are *wilkom* to stay with me at the house as long as you need," she offered.

"Thank you, that's very kind." David turned toward Liam. "We just need a few minutes to clean up the kitchen and to get *Mammi* Ruth settled."

"It won't take long," she added.

Liam blew out a breath, then nodded. "Okay, fine. I'll drive you both to see the damage, and then to the Amish Shoppe. But you can't disturb the area, David. It's considered a crime scene, at least until the cause of the fire has been determined. An arson investigator from

Fond du Lac has already been called out. He'll be able to tell us for sure what happened."

"That is very helpful." David managed a grim smile. "I know it sounds strange, but it doesn't seem real until I see for myself."

"*Komm*, Liam. You'll have coffee while you wait, *ja*?"

"Thanks Elizabeth." Liam followed her and David inside.

Once she had *Mammi* Ruth settled upstairs, she returned to the kitchen to find David had finished the dishes. Liam's expression held concern, and she knew he was worried about David's lack of insurance.

She wished for David's sake that he'd kept his policy, too. She considered approaching Bishop Bachman about David's home, although she doubted the community would rally around him.

"Elizabeth, would you prefer if I spend tonight at my workshop?"

"*Ach*, no, why would you think that?" She was puzzled by his question.

"I'm trying to decide if my being here is causing you and *Mammi* Ruth more harm than good." He blew out a breath. "I don't want to bring danger here, yet I don't want to leave you and Ruth alone, either."

"I can make up my own mind, *ja*?" She couldn't help feeling defensive. Why did men always think they knew best? She was perfectly capable of running her own business, and her life. "I prefer to have you stay, David, but certain sure the choice is yours."

"For what it's worth, I think you should stay here at Elizabeth's, too. For her safety and yours," Liam said. "Although the offer to move everyone to my place still stands."

"*Mammi* Ruth will be more comfortable here, close to the Amish women who stop in to visit." Elizabeth couldn't imagine her mother-in-law wanting to move to a different place, especially one owned by an *Englischer*.

The house was Adam's and therefore would always be her home.

"Okay, we'll leave things the way they are," David said slowly. "But if you change your mind, let me know."

She wouldn't, but appreciated his willingness to follow her wishes. David had once again folded the quilt and tucked it beneath the pillow. He seemed determined not to cause her additional work, going as far as to help with kitchen chores as well as cutting wood for the stove. The main level was neat and tidy by the time she was finished pulling back her hair and tucking it beneath her *kapp*.

"Ready?" Liam asked.

"Of course." She preceded David and Liam outside. David opened the passenger door for her, then slid in the back.

The ride to David's took them past the Amish Shoppe. When Liam pulled up in front of the charred wood that was all that remained of David's home, she couldn't tear her gaze away from the terrible sight.

If David had been there...she couldn't finish the thought.

"Wow," David murmured. "It's worse than I anticipated."

"I can turn around and take you to the Amish shops," Liam said quickly.

"No, I want to walk around." David quickly pushed out of the back seat. She decided to go with him, in case he needed support.

He'd been there for her, more times than she could count over these past few days. The least she could do was to return the favor.

David stood for a long moment, so stoic and solemn, that she couldn't help but tuck her hand in the crook of his arm.

She'd stay at his side for as long as he needed her.

* * *

The damage to his home, the one he'd built with his own hands, hit hard. Granted he'd thought of selling, especially recently, but this?

His home being destroyed by arson wasn't part of the plan.

Sure, the land was still worth something, but it was a crippling blow just the same.

It would take selling furniture for a year to save up enough to rebuild. And doing the work would take time away from his business.

If not for Elizabeth's hand on his arm, he might have fallen to his knees in despair. Instead, he drew in a deep breath and walked. He didn't hurry, for Elizabeth's sake, since she still limped a bit due to her swollen knee, but he headed through the snow to the perimeter of his property. The area appeared undisturbed, until he reached the southwest corner. He stopped abruptly when he found a set of footprints in the snow.

"Liam? Check this out." He gestured for the sheriff to come over.

Liam knelt by the footprints, then slowly stood. "These could belong to the arsonist, or they could have been left by someone out hiking."

"Hiking? On private property in the snow a

week before Christmas?" David snorted. "Try again."

"Look, it's suspicious, sure. But they're also not proof of any wrongdoing." Liam pulled out his cell phone and took several photos of the footprints. "I'll keep the information on file, but don't expect them to break the case open anytime soon."

"I don't expect that," David said, trying not to sound as hopeless as he felt.

"Finding something is better than nothing, ain't so?" Elizabeth murmured.

"Yes." After finishing the walk around his property, he stood once more surveying the remains of his house. It was difficult not to give in to stark feeling of despair. He'd built it after relocating here from Madison, pouring all his energy into creating the dwelling.

"Hey, you'll be okay." Liam rested his hand on his back. "Shauna and I will help."

"I can ask Bishop Bachman for volunteers, to help you rebuild, too," Elizabeth offered.

That surprised him, although he didn't hold out much hope that the Amish community would come together for an outsider. "Thanks, but it's not an Amish problem, or yours, Liam." David had no intention of taking Liam and Shauna's money. "Although I may need some help from Shauna in running the store when it's time to rebuild."

Liam nodded. "She has one more semester to go until she finishes her bachelor's degree. Before moving to Green Lake, she worked full-time while attending school part-time. She's used to keeping busy. I'm sure she'll gladly pitch in to help."

He forced himself to turn away from the wreckage. "You haven't learned anything else about the shooter?"

"No, but keep in mind it's only been two days. Things don't happen overnight the way they do on TV."

He hadn't watched TV since getting out of jail, but knew what Liam meant. No point in expecting quick answers.

"*Komm*, we should get to the Amish Shoppe, *ja*?" Elizabeth said.

"Sure." He glanced at Liam, who nodded. They headed toward Liam's SUV.

He expected the Saturday shopping day to be busy, but thought about ducking out for an hour or so to head over to the Green Lake Grill. He decided not to mention his plan to Liam, instinctively knowing he wouldn't approve. How he'd get there, he wasn't sure. He may need to see if he could borrow Shauna's car.

"Would Shauna have time to help today?" David asked Liam. "Or is she working on exams?"

"No exams. She'll have to retake her business law class in the spring." Liam nodded thoughtfully. "I'll ask her to stop by."

"Thanks." He noticed Elizabeth frowning, as if she suspected he had an ulterior motive.

He didn't like keeping secrets from her. Or from Liam. But a quick trip to the Green Lake Grill wasn't that big a deal. And likely wouldn't give him any additional information.

Yet he had to try. His house was gone, and he needed to do something about getting to the bottom of this.

"Liam, do you think there's a possibility the Amish Shoppe could be targeted, too?" Elizabeth asked.

His gut clenched. Liam met his gaze in the rearview mirror.

"I've already arranged for my deputies to keep an eye on the place. And, Elizabeth, don't be upset, but I posted some cameras on the outside of the building too. They're small enough that no one should notice."

"*Ach*, that's not our way, Liam." Her brow furrowed. "If the elders knew, they might not allow us to work there, ain't so?"

"The cameras are temporary," Liam insisted. "You saw what was left after David's house burned down. Think about the impact to all of the Amish who sell their goods at the barn."

Elizabeth didn't say anything, and David could tell she was torn between being true to her Amish roots and wanting to keep the Amish Shoppe safe.

He understood her dilemma. He felt the same way.

Liam's phone rang, and he used the hands-free function to respond. "Harland."

"It's Garrett. I have a witness who claims he saw an Amish man near the location of the fire."

Elizabeth gasped and put a hand to her mouth.

"A reliable witness?" Liam asked.

"From what I can tell, she has no reason to lie. Her name is Melody Jenkins and she's a marathon runner. She states she was heading down the highway past David's house, when she saw him."

"Before or after the fire?"

"Before the fire, or she would have called it in. She was certain the guy was tall, wearing Amish dress including the hat, but she didn't get a good enough look to determine if he wore a beard. I've emailed her statement, including her number if you'd like to follow up."

"Thanks, that's helpful." Liam disconnected from the call.

"Jacob is tall," David pointed out.

"Yes, but eyewitness testimony isn't perfect," Liam countered. "Terms like short and tall are rather subjective and come solely from the witness's perspective."

"Amish dress the same," Elizabeth pointed out. "Certain sure it could have been anyone."

"I know." David understood he shouldn't jump to conclusions. Yet he still saw Jacob Strauss as a potential suspect.

Liam dropped them off at the Amish Shoppe and David escorted Elizabeth down the center aisle. He was glad she'd insisted on coming with him: her presence had helped keep him calm.

"Let's hope we see many customers, today, *ja*?"

"Absolutely." He squeezed her hand, then stepped back to wait until she was inside her quilt shop. When she was settled, he turned to unlock his showroom.

As predicted, the crowds came early and, thankfully, spent money. He was pleased to have sold a dresser that had been on his showroom floor for almost three months. A very good day, even if he didn't sell anything more.

He was so busy he forgot about the Green Lake Grill, until Shauna arrived.

"Uncle Davy, this place is packed," she exclaimed. "I hear you need help."

"In more ways than one," he agreed. Glancing at the time, he realized it was past noon. "I'm going to get lunch for Elizabeth. Do you want something?"

"No, I ate before I came." She waved her hand. "Go ahead, I'll take over from here."

"Shauna, I have a favor to ask. Would you let me borrow your car to run an errand? I won't be gone long."

"Of course." Without hesitation, she dropped her car keys into the palm of his hand. He knew Liam had purchased the car for her as a wedding gift, after her previous one had been totaled. "Davy, you do have a driver's license, right?"

"Yes." That was true. He hadn't given up his driver's license, more so to use as an ID if needed. "I'll be back shortly."

He headed toward the Sunshine Café and ordered lunch for two. He delivered the sandwich to Elizabeth.

"*Denke*, David. *Sehr gut* to be so busy."

"Yes, very much so." He wanted to stay and eat with her, but more customers came in, so he decided to eat later. He stored the sandwich in his workroom cooler, then headed out to find Shauna's car.

Once he was settled behind the wheel, doubts assailed him. Was it worth leaving their busiest day to find the Green Lake Grill?

Then again, it not today, then when? Tomorrow was Sunday, and he wouldn't have the opportunity to borrow Shauna's car. Then the Amish Shoppe was closed until Wednesday morning.

No, he had to do this. He took a moment to familiarize himself with the controls, since he hadn't been behind the wheel in two years. Then he put the gearshift in Reverse and carefully backed out of the parking lot.

He took it slow, heading to the downtown area of Green Lake. There weren't that many restaurants in the area, so he figured he'd find it eventually.

It wasn't located in the downtown area, so he widened his search, taking the main highway around the lake. He found it tucked off the highway a bit, near a wooded area. The place was rustic, and somewhat worn down. He remembered Shauna mentioning a rough crowd when she and Liam had stopped in.

Interesting, because the restaurant was situated so that there was a nice view of the lake.

He parked, slid out from behind the wheel and tucked his hands in his coat pockets as he walked inside.

Surprisingly, the interior was dark, as if half the lights didn't work. And the furnishings were dingy and worn, too. He thought the owners might have gotten complacent, which was why the business was attracting a rough crowd.

He stood in the doorway for a long moment, scanning the crowd. Despite being in poor repair, the place was busy. Maybe because it was a Saturday afternoon.

It occurred to him that the rough crowd might come in at nighttime, rather than the middle of the day. He didn't see anyone he recognized. His memory of what Carson Wells had looked like before he'd died was clear as daylight in his mind, but that wasn't helpful now.

"Table for one?" A woman approached holding a menu.

"Ah, no, thank you. I'm looking for a friend." He was conscious of his Amish clothing, although it wasn't that noticeable beneath his coat.

The woman shrugged and moved away.

David moved to the side, still raking his gaze over the restaurant patrons. After a few minutes, he felt foolish. It wasn't as if the gunman and/or arsonist would walk up to him and introduce himself.

He turned away. Liam had mentioned checking the place out, and he figured it was better to let the local authorities handle this.

And really, if the arsonist was Amish as noted by the witness, then it wasn't likely he would be hanging out here at an *Englisch* restaurant.

Hunching his shoulders against the wind, David turned to gaze out at the lake. The snow-covered trees and the icy water were beautiful in a stark way.

He turned to head back to Shauna's car, when he heard the restaurant door close. Glancing over his shoulder, he was startled to see a stocky man with a ski mask on, standing there with a gun.

No! David tucked his chin to his chest and hit the ground, rolling toward the vehicle mere seconds before a muffled shot rang out. He crawled beneath the car, desperate for cover. Then noticed a pair of boots running past. David scooted forward, peering from beneath the car in time to see a black truck roar out of sight.

He closed his eyes for a moment, realizing the gunman had been inside the Green Lake Grill, after all.

EIGHT

After wrapping up a Christmas quilt, Elizabeth took a moment to rest and eat the sandwich David had brought from Leah's Sunshine Café. There was a lull in the shopping, although she had nothing to complain about.

Her sales had been brisk, and she noticed several customers checking out David's furniture, too.

It made her sad to think about how he'd lost his home. Although, if she were honest, she'd admit to being glad to have a good reason to have him sleep in her living room for the next few days.

Mammi Ruth couldn't be upset at him staying when he had nowhere else to go. Well, technically he did have somewhere else to go. He could stay with Liam, but she didn't need to know that.

"Elizabeth?" Shauna's expression was full of concern.

She immediately rose to her feet. "What's wrong?"

"David is fine," Shauna hastened to assure her. "But a gunman took a shot at him at the Green Lake Grill. Liam is there, now. I felt you should know."

"The Green Lake Grill?" Elizabeth frowned. "What is David doing there? I thought he was in the workroom?"

A flash of guilt shadowed Shauna's features. "He asked to borrow my car, so I gave him my keys. I didn't have any idea that he planned to go to the Green Lake Grill."

"He drove your car?" Stunned at the revelation, she could only stare at Shauna. She'd thought David had chosen to live like the Amish, but mayhap she was wrong.

And she really didn't like the way David had kept this little side trip of his a secret. It reminded her of how Adam had kept things from her. Always saying for her to mind her own business when she asked where he was going or what he was doing.

"David has his driver's license, so I didn't think too much about loaning him the car." Shauna grimaced. "I guess that goes against your beliefs, though."

She didn't answer, her thoughts whirling. "Certain sure he's not injured?"

"Yes, Liam said he's fine. He hit the ground and scrambled beneath the car." Shauna reached out to touch her hand. "David will be here soon. In the meantime, I have to continue helping in the showroom." Shauna turned away.

Elizabeth resumed her seat and picked up her half-eaten sandwich. Unfortunately, she'd lost her appetite. Wasting food was frowned upon, so she forced herself to take one bite, then another.

Another customer came in, so she gratefully set the last quarter of her sandwich aside. Keeping busy would help her ignore the keen sense of betrayal.

In truth, David's driving wasn't that great a sin. During *Rumspringa*, Amish teenagers were known to drive cars as they had their taste of *Englisch* life. The custom was such so that the children would choose being baptized as Amish on their own, without being forced.

Her real disappointment came from David's doing so without telling her.

It was almost an hour later before David and Liam returned. Liam's expression was grave, and there was a touch of guilt in David's eyes as he looked at her.

"I'm sorry, Elizabeth. I hope you're not upset with me."

She managed a smile. "I'm glad you weren't hurt, David. Did you get a good description of the man who shot at you?"

"He wore a ski mask," David said. "Although he was shorter and stockier in build, like the guy I saw here inside the Amish Shoppe that first night."

"I have Garrett and another deputy questioning the Green Lake Grill staff," Liam added. "But so far, no one has come forward with a name."

Shauna threw her arms around David. "I'm so glad you're okay, Davy."

"I'm fine." David awkwardly patted her back. "And thankfully, your car wasn't hit by a stray bullet, either."

"As if I care about that," Shauna said. "You're all that matters."

Elizabeth watched them, wondering if David was feeling pulled back into the *Englisch* world. The thought saddened her, and she realized in that moment just how much she'd cherished their friendship.

Their companionship.

What if David decided to go with his family, rather than continuing his current path where he'd once intended to join the Amish?

She felt hot, then cold. She returned to her quilt shop, telling herself that it didn't matter what David decided.

After all, she'd already informed him marriage was not for her. She was sure she and David could still be friends, regardless of which path he decided to take.

The next few hours passed by quickly. When closing time grew near, she straightened her stock, grateful to note that she only had one Christmas quilt left.

She would start making more next fall, after the summer wedding quilt rush.

Yet keeping focused on the success of her business didn't help lift her spirits.

"Elizabeth, Shauna would like to drive us back to your house," David said, his tone tentative. His blue gaze searched hers for a long moment. "Unless you've changed your mind about having me sleep on your sofa."

"*Ach*, of course not. You're *wilkom* to stay." It seemed uncharitable to refuse him after the way his home had been burned to the ground. The disappointment she felt was her problem, not his. "*Denke*, a ride home would be *sehr gut*."

"Great. Are you ready to go?" David glanced around her tidy shop.

She nodded and locked the door before following him to the showroom where Shauna waited. There was no sign of Liam.

"Oh, and I have a padlock for your barn." David held up the device. "I hope you don't mind, but I'd feel safer if you kept the doors locked."

"That's fine." Having the sturdy lock would give her one less thing to worry about. She followed Shauna and David down the center aisle toward the front door.

Outside, she glanced up at the eaves but didn't see the small cameras Liam had mentioned. Maybe installing the cameras was for the best. She truly didn't want the building to burn the way David's house had.

Had the arsonist really been Amish? She didn't want to believe it, despite what the witness had seen.

Yet, there was no denying the danger was very real. David had clearly been targeted.

And her, too? If so, she wished she understood the motive behind it.

She didn't doubt David would keep her and *Mammi* Ruth safe. But she needed to try to keep a bit of emotional distance from him, too.

Her bruised feelings indicated she'd already allowed David to get too close.

* * *

David sensed Elizabeth was upset with him, and thought he understood why. After giving up electronics and other worldly goods, he'd broken the rules by driving Shauna's car.

In hindsight, he couldn't even be that sorry about it. He was glad he'd been alone at the Green Lake Grill, rather than risk Shauna or Liam.

But other than his belief the stocky man he'd seen today was the same one who'd picked the lock to gain access to the Amish Shoppe, he hadn't discovered anything useful.

Well, except for knowing the Green Lake Grill was being patronized by criminals.

Liam hadn't sounded confident about learning anything more about the gunman. Everything had happened so fast that David couldn't even say for certain if the guy had been wearing Amish clothing.

His gaze had focused on the man's face, covered with a black ski mask. He firmly believed the gunman had recognized him in the entranceway of the restaurant and had decided to come after him.

In broad daylight. Had the gunman known no one inside would rat him out?

"Are you okay?" Shauna's voice betrayed her concern.

"Fine." He needed to shake it off. Although in his mind's eye, he was thinking about that table in the back where the three men were sitting.

Had one of them been the stocky guy? Difficult to say. He wished he had a phone with a camera so he could have taken a picture.

So much for living the simple life of the Amish, he thought grimly.

Shauna pulled up in front of Elizabeth's house and slid the gearshift into Park. "I wish I had a way of getting in touch with you, Davy."

"No need, we'll be safe here." He slid out of the back seat and opened Elizabeth's door. "Tomorrow is Sunday, and I'm sure things will be quiet."

"Denke." Elizabeth held her bag of sewing close to her body as she turned to bid Shauna goodbye. "Take care, *ja*?"

"You, too." Shauna waved and waited for them to go inside the house before driving off.

"Excuse me while I check on *Mammi* Ruth." Elizabeth didn't meet his gaze as she hurried upstairs.

He tried not to be disheartened by her anger. After adding wood to the fire, he went into the kitchen to check on dinner. Elizabeth had left beef and vegetable soup on the counter, so he set it on the woodstove to get hot.

She also had fresh bread and butter, which he set on the table, too.

Elizabeth returned after fifteen minutes. "*Mammi* Ruth would prefer a tray in her room for dinner."

"She's upset with me, too, huh?" David's attempt to lighten things up fell flat.

"No, she is feeling weak, that's all." Elizabeth stirred the soup for a moment.

"I know you're angry, but I'm hoping you'll find it in your heart to forgive me." She'd forgiven him for killing a man; certainly driving a car wasn't nearly as terrible. Granted he hadn't intended to kill Carson Wells.

And he had fully intended to drive Shauna's car.

"I'm not angry." The way she avoided his gaze belied her words. "'Tis your choice to make, ain't so?"

"My choice to drive Shauna's car," he agreed.

She set the top on the kettle of soup with a loud clatter. "Your choice to go to the Green Lake Grill in the first place, without telling me."

Now he understood. "You are right, Elizabeth. I should have informed you of my intent," he admitted. "After seeing what was left of my house, I needed to do something, anything, to find the man responsible."

"*Ach*, for what purpose?" She turned to face him. "To seek revenge?"

"No! Only so that he could be arrested." He rubbed the back of his head, where the lump was slowly getting smaller. "I don't want to be in a situation where I'm responsible for another man's death." Having Carson Wells's demise hanging over him like a shroud was bad enough.

"I see." He couldn't tell if she truly believed him. "Well, I must get *Mammi* Ruth's meal ready, ain't so?"

He felt rather useless standing there. "I'll put the lock on the barn door, if that's okay."

"Certain sure." She filled a bowl with steaming soup and then added two slices of bread. When she headed back upstairs, he pulled on his coat, took the padlock from his pocket and walked outside.

It seemed like days, rather than hours, since he'd been out chopping wood. Glancing around, he didn't see anything amiss. He strode straight to the barn door and yanked it open. He didn't see anyone inside, so he closed it and attached the sturdy padlock.

At least now they didn't have to worry about anyone hiding in there, waiting to attack.

Yet as he trudged back inside, he knew the danger was far from over. Either an Amish man or an English one had tried to kill him.

More than once.

He needed to figure out a way to find the man responsible, before he could try again.

Elizabeth was filling large bowls of soup for them when he returned. He joined her at the table, then reached over to take her hand. She stared at their clasped hands for a moment, then bowed her head.

"Dear Lord, we ask You to bless this amazing food. We also ask for You to continue keeping us safe in Your care. And please, Lord, forgive my sins. Amen."

"Please forgive my sins, too. Amen," Elizabeth echoed. When she lifted her head, her warm brown gaze met his. "We are all sinners, *ja*?"

"Yes." Some more so than others, he thought wearily. Unfortunately, his list of sins seemed to be growing, rather than shrinking.

"You'll still attend services with us tomorrow morning?" Elizabeth's question drew him from his thoughts.

"Yes, I'd like that."

"Sehr gut." Elizabeth smiled, which felt like the first warmth he'd felt from her since he'd left the Amish Shoppe in Shauna's car.

"Are there other chores that need tending tomorrow?" He knew the Amish didn't work on Sunday, but chores were obviously an exception.

"Nothing pressing. You've brought more than enough firewood in, ain't so?"

"I can chop more, too, as needed." It occurred to him that he may want to stock up the woodpile for her. Once Liam had arrested the gunman, there would be no need for him to continue staying here.

No matter how much he wanted to.

They finished eating, then worked together to take care of the dishes. He was glad some of their previous camaraderie had returned.

He hoped that meant she'd forgiven him.

After Elizabeth bid him good-night, he stretched out on the sofa beneath her wonderfully soft quilt and closed his eyes.

Immediately the stocky, masked gunman flashed in his mind.

David turned to prayer, seeking peace from the disturbing events of the day. He prayed Liam would find the man responsible, and he prayed for Elizabeth's safety.

Finally, he relaxed enough to drift off.

A muffled thump woke him, and he frowned in the darkness, wondering if he'd imagined it. Then he tensed. What if the stocky gunman had found him here?

He couldn't take that risk. He shoved the quilt aside, quickly slipped on his boots, coat and hat, then silently crept to the front door. Remembering the incident in the barn, he went back to grab a log from the woodpile. He'd use it to frighten an intruder or to block a blow, rather than to strike. Then he opened the door and stepped outside.

The moon reflected off the snow, providing enough light for him to see better than he'd expected. He silently closed the door behind him, then stood for a moment, sweeping his gaze over the front yard.

After finding nothing out of place, he moved to the left, the side of the house where he thought the thudding sound had come from. It also happened to be the same side of the house where he'd noticed the two pairs of footprints in the snow earlier in the week. At the corner, he hesitated, then poked his head around to see if anyone was there.

The area was empty. Then his gaze narrowed as he noticed the snow seemed disturbed beneath one of the windows.

Still holding the stick of firewood, he moved along the side of the house. There were blue cellar doors leading into the space beneath the house, where he knew Elizabeth stored freshly canned goods and other food items. After rounding that, he paused near the window. Peering through the glass, he frowned as he realized the entire living space was visible.

If someone had stood there looking in, they'd have seen him stretched out on the sofa.

Panic gripped him by the throat. Had the thudding noise been a diversion? A way to draw him out so the intruder could get inside?

He pushed away from the house and ran back around to the front door. He took the corner too fast, his boots slipping in the snow. Somehow, he managed to stay upright, pushing off the wall as he rushed to the front door and threw it open.

Elizabeth was standing there, a shawl wrapped tightly around her. "David? *Ach*, what are you doing outside in the middle of the night?" Her gaze landed on the quarter log of wood in his hand. "Are you bringing in more wood?"

"No." He dropped the log on the top of the pile near the woodburning stove. "Are you okay? You didn't see anyone come in?" He pulled her to his side, while raking his gaze over the room. Had there been enough time for the intruder to duck inside and hide? He couldn't say for sure.

"I heard the front door close and came down to find you were gone." She stared at him with wide eyes. "Why would you think someone might come inside?"

"I heard a muffled thud," he admitted. "Stay here, while I look around."

"Look around?" Now she sounded exasperated. "No one is here but us, David."

"I hope so." His heart thudded painfully against his sternum as he moved through the house, peering into closets and behind large furniture.

Finally, he forced himself to stop being so paranoid. He blew out a breath and returned to the main living area. "I think we're safe."

"Safe from whom? Did you see someone outside?"

"No, but there were several footprints in the snow by the window." He gestured to the one. "I think someone may have been out there, looking in."

"Footprints," she whispered. "Like the ones I followed the night I was pushed to the ground."

"Yes." He longed to draw her into his arms,

but reminded himself they were only friends. After the events earlier in the day, she wouldn't want anything more from him. "I'm sorry if I frightened you. I was afraid someone had drawn me out on purpose to get to you."

Her gaze softened and she stepped close, putting her hand on his arm. "I'm safe with you, David."

"Are you?" His tone was full of doubt. "I'm not so sure."

"I am." She surprised him by coming closer still. He gently drew her into his arms, intending to offer comfort.

But their embrace was so much more. Elizabeth felt right in his arms, as if God had made them for each other.

Yet he knew that wasn't true. God would never pair a woman like Elizabeth with a sinner like him.

NINE

Elizabeth didn't know why she'd hugged David. Mayhap it was his unique scent mixed with sawdust that drew her in. But as much as she liked being held in his arms, so different than what she'd experienced with Adam, she knew there could be nothing between them.

She reluctantly pulled away, reminding herself that David was a friend, one who had withheld the truth earlier that day.

"I'm sorry if I overstepped," David said softly.

She bit back a flash of impatience. "We are friends, *ja*?"

"Elizabeth!" *Mammi* Ruth's shrill voice interrupted their conversation. "Help!"

She frowned. "Excuse me. I must see what she needs."

"Of course." David's low, husky voice sent a

ripple of awareness down her spine. She didn't understand why she was so drawn to this man.

She tried to put her strange feelings aside as she hurried to the second floor. When she found *Mammi* Ruth on the floor, she gasped. "*Ach*, what happened?"

"I fell trying to return to bed from the bathroom." *Mammi* Ruth's face was drawn and pale. "I can't get up."

Elizabeth knew she wouldn't be able to lift the woman on her own. She went to the top of the stairs. "David? We need you."

"Coming!" True to his word, he swiftly mounted the stairs, concern darkening his blue eyes. "Are you all right?"

"Please help me get her back to bed." Elizabeth felt terrible for not understanding how weak the older woman had become.

"Of course." David strode into the room and without hesitation, bent down and scooped *Mammi* Ruth up from the floor. He didn't indicate she was too heavy, as he gently set her down on the bed.

"*Denke*, David." She rested her hand on his arm, wishing she could hug him again. "I'll take it from here."

"Any time." He nodded at *Mammi* Ruth,

then turned away to give them the privacy they needed.

"Are you hurt?" Elizabeth asked. "Do we need to go to the hospital?"

"I'm fine," *Mammi* Ruth said with a sigh. "I became dizzy but still tried to get back to bed on my own."

"*Ach*, it's a good thing David was here to help." Elizabeth tucked one of her quilts around the elder woman. "Certain sure I wouldn't have been able to get you up alone."

Mammi Ruth frowned but didn't say anything more. Elizabeth knew accepting help from an *Englischer* wasn't something the elder woman would have normally done. Yet *Mammi* Ruth likely understood she'd still be on the floor if not for David's presence.

"*Denke*, Elizabeth," *Mammi* Ruth said as she closed her eyes. The woman's gratitude was a rare gift, and Elizabeth lightly patted her arm.

"*Wilkom*. Now rest, *ja*? And call before you get up on your own."

Elizabeth went back down to the first floor to thank David, but when she found him resting on the sofa, she quietly returned to her room.

Sleep eluded her as memories of David's embrace swirled in her mind. By morning, she'd convinced herself she'd overreacted to the entire situation.

But after checking on *Mammi* Ruth, she walked down the stairs to find David had already stoked the fire and was making coffee.

"*Ach*, I can do that," she protested.

"So can I," he responded, smiling at her over his shoulder. "The rule should be the first one up makes coffee, don't you think?"

"Certain sure others would not agree," she said lightly. His actions weren't the usual routine among the Amish, which made her wonder if David was doing all of this simply to impress her. And whether everything would change if a deeper relationship developed between them.

Reminding herself she wasn't interested in anything beyond her current friendship with David didn't seem to help. Her mind betrayed her by coming up with what-if scenarios.

Shaking off her thoughts, she set about making breakfast. As she filled a tray with food, she glanced at David. "I'll ask *Mammi* Ruth if she still wishes to attend services with us."

"I'm happy to help her walk, if needed." He gestured to the tray. "Would you like me to carry that for you?"

"*Ach*, no, it's best if I take care of it." She lifted the tray. "I'll be back soon, *ja*?"

David nodded, and she hurried away. The process took longer than anticipated, as *Mammi* Ruth wanted help getting to the bathroom again, before settling in her chair to eat.

When she returned to the kitchen, David had completed the rest of the meal, putting the food on plates for both of them.

"Denke," she murmured, taking her seat. She reached for his hand and bowed her head. "Lord, we thank You for the gift of food, and for keeping us safe in Your loving arms, amen."

"Amen," David added. *"Mammi* Ruth is doing okay after her tumble?"

"Ja." Elizabeth smiled wearily. "And she still wishes to attend church services. Today's gathering will be at the Moore home."

"Leah's family?" David brightened. "That sounds nice."

After they finished breakfast, David helped her with the dishes. Then he went out to carry in more firewood while she helped *Mammi* Ruth get dressed.

"Mayhap you need to walk more to keep up your strength." Elizabeth wasn't sure that staying in her room so much was good for her.

"Ach, I'll try." The woman seemed to take her suggestion to heart.

Their progress down the stairs to the main

level was slow, but steady. David offered his arm, and *Mammi* Ruth graciously accepted his support.

The Moore home wasn't too far. When they arrived, Leah welcomed them in and showed them to the living area. Extra seating had been provided by the men.

As usual, the men were gathered in one area, the women in another. She noticed Jacob was in attendance. Not that she'd expected him to avoid services. Bishop Bachman was in discussion with several of the elders. She hoped to find a few moments alone with Bishop Bachman after services and before the elders went to discuss community business. David escorted *Mammi* Ruth toward a seat next to several other women, then moved away to chat with some of the other men in attendance.

She scanned the crowd, noticing the bishop had finished his conversation. Was now a good time to talk to him?

"Elizabeth?" She'd been so intent on seeking counsel with Bishop Bachman that she hadn't noticed Luke Embers approach.

"Hello, Luke." She greeted Adam's cousin with a smile.

"It's good to see you. How have you been doing since Adam's passing?"

"Sehr gut." She found it difficult to appear as if she were still mourning Adam's death. "Business at the quilt shop keeps me busy, *ja*?"

"Yes, I have heard your quilts sell very well," Luke said kindly. "But what about the renovations Adam was making in your upstairs bedrooms? Have you been up there recently? Has anyone been working on them for you?"

Adam must have told Luke about the renovations, but she still found his question strange. "No, I don't have any plans to resume the work for now. Mayhap in the spring."

"I see." Luke's gaze was intense. "Would you allow me to escort you home after the gathering meal?"

Escort her home? Why was he asking her to do something that would appear as if they were courting? Luke was several years younger than her, and she had never been a source of interest to him before.

"Not today," she demurred. It wasn't easy to refuse him outright, but she wasn't about to accept his offer, either. "I will let you know if I change my mind about the renovations, *ja*?" Without waiting for Luke to respond, she turned away, quickly joining *Mammi* Ruth and the others.

Concentrating on Bishop Bachman's sermon

and the songs was difficult as Luke's question reverberated through her mind.

It didn't make sense that Luke or Jacob would show an interest in her, when they had never looked at her twice before. Jacob had been married to Anna, while Luke had been seen walking with Rebecca last fall. Although it could be that Rebecca had lost interest in Luke. She wouldn't know, because she didn't waste time keeping up on community gossip.

The way he'd asked about the renovations, which had sat idle for months now, niggled at her. She felt certain that Luke was asking for some other reason than being concerned for her welfare.

Yet she couldn't imagine what his motive might be.

David had noticed the younger man talking to Elizabeth but hadn't been close enough to hear what he'd said. He focused on Bishop Bachman's voice, enjoying the cadence and rhythm since he couldn't understand everything the elder man said in Pennsylvania Dutch. And he enjoyed the singing of hymns, too.

He thought about trying to get a moment alone with the bishop to express his desire to become Amish, but his past held him back. Did he deserve such grace? Perhaps not.

After eating the noon meal, it was time to clean up and head home. He joined the men in removing the extra seating, while Elizabeth worked with the women to take care of the food.

Mammi Ruth leaned heavily on his arm as they walked back. He glanced at Elizabeth, hoping she'd understand his concern. She frowned and nodded.

"I'll help you get upstairs to your room," he offered.

"Denke," Mammi Ruth whispered. Elizabeth followed them up, then took over the caretaking.

When she joined him in the living room, he could tell she was concerned. "Do you think she'll be able to stay home alone once we go back to work at the Amish Shoppe?"

"Ach, certain sure I can ask for assistance. Mary Moore, Leah's mother, has already offered to stop in each day."

"That would help," he agreed. "Did you get a chance to talk to Bishop Bachman?"

"No." She frowned. "I attempted to do so, but he was busy. I wanted to ask about the Amish helping to rebuild your house, too. But as Jacob stayed away, I felt there was no need to bother him immediately. Although that was before Luke Embers, Adam's cousin, approached and asked me to walk home with him."

"He did?" David shouldn't have been surprised. She was an attractive woman.

"Yes, but it doesn't matter." She shrugged. "I will not change my mind about courting either man."

"Of course, your wishes should be honored," he agreed. Still, he wondered about the two men showing interest so closely together. Then again, he wasn't privy to Amish courting rituals. "Is there something I can do for you?"

"*Ach*, most of our chores have been done, *ja*?" She watched him closely. "What would you do if you were at home?"

"I would probably work," he said in a low voice. "I know that is viewed as wrong but keeping busy is important for me. Otherwise, I spend too much time in my thoughts, dwelling on the mistakes I've made in the past."

"Certain sure we have all made mistakes."

"Not all mistakes are considered equal," he argued. "A man died because of my inability to control my anger."

"*Ja*, loss of life is serious, but so are many sins. And God knows what is in your heart, David."

"I hope so." He stared down at his hands for a moment, seeing the bloody knuckles he'd experienced six years ago, then quickly rose to his feet. "I'd like to take a walk outside for a bit, if you don't mind."

"Of course." She regarded him thoughtfully, but didn't press him for more.

David swept a keen eye over the area as he strolled around Elizabeth's property. He wasn't entirely sure where her property ended and Jacob's took over.

The Amish didn't draw those sorts of lines in the sand; they were all about sharing among the community.

A way of life that would have benefited those outside the Amish community, as well.

There were cows and horses in the pasture, and he noticed an old rusty manual plow partially covered with snow near Jacob's barn. Nothing else looked out of place, though, so he kept walking.

Upon reaching Elizabeth's barn, he examined the ground carefully but didn't find any additional footprints indicating someone had been there recently. The padlock he'd placed also appeared undisturbed.

Small comfort, he thought as pulled the key from his pocket and unlocked the door. He did a quick check of the interior, finding nothing amiss. After securing the padlock, he moved on.

The barn was a large structure, and as he walked around it, he thought about how Elizabeth had given away the livestock. He wondered if that meant that come spring, the barn would be lifted off its concrete floor and moved to another location, too.

The Amish didn't let anything go to waste. Another admirable trait he wished more people would adapt.

His thoughts veered toward the fire that had destroyed his house. He wanted to ask Liam if he'd found anything more from the shooting incident at the Green Lake Grill, but without a phone or a horse and buggy, the only way to get information would be to walk into town.

Not that he minded walking, but that meant leaving Elizabeth and Ruth alone. Something he wasn't willing to do.

As he rounded the barn, he saw a tall man standing outside the neighboring house about thirty yards away. David eased closer to the edge of the barn, hiding himself as he tried to see the man's features more clearly.

The guy was tall, and when the man began to pace impatiently back and forth, David caught a glimpse of his face. No surprise, he recognized him as Jacob.

His behavior was odd, though. Why was he walking around outside his own home? Then David saw a second man approach.

Like Jacob, he wore Amish clothing. The collar of his coat made it difficult to see his face, but he appeared younger and he did not have a beard, indicating he was not married. For sure the newcomer was shorter than Jacob, by a good four to five inches. But the guy didn't have the same stocky build as the man he'd chased through the Amish Shoppe that first night.

There were no trees or other places to seek cover between Elizabeth's barn and the area where Jacob and the other man stood, so he couldn't get any closer to see exactly what they were doing.

Jacob was scowling, although from what David could tell that was hardly unusual. He'd never seen Jacob smile. The second man stood a few feet away from Jacob as if he didn't want to get too close.

"What do you think you're doing?" Jacob's harsh tone traveled across the distance, loud enough for David to hear.

"What do you care?" the second man asked. "I can court whomever I choose."

It occurred to David they were speaking English, which was a bit unusual. Then again, the language was more commonly used among the younger Amish who interacted with the public.

To his knowledge, Jacob didn't interact with the public. He only ran his farm, sharing the proceeds with the Amish community, not selling his goods in a store.

At that moment the second man turned just enough that David could see his face. His pulse spiked as he recognized Luke Embers, the man who'd asked to escort Elizabeth home from services.

Adam's cousin was talking to Adam's best friend. Something wasn't right here. Should he go out and confront them?

"Leave Elizabeth alone," Jacob said sternly.

"Why, so you can have her?" Luke asked, a slight sneer in his tone. "Is this really why you wanted to talk to me? To discuss Elizabeth? I thought you were interested in doing business."

"Leave her alone, Luke," Jacob repeated. Then he turned and strode back up to the house.

Luke stood still for a moment, before turning to leave as well. David eased around the barn, watching as the younger man headed over to his horse and buggy parked in the driveway. Moments later, Luke was gone.

The interchange had been centered on Elizabeth. Yet he found it telling that the discussion had been so clinical. *Stay away from Elizabeth*, Jacob had said, not because he liked or cared for her, but just a command to stay away. And Luke's response, claiming he could court whomever he wanted, had lacked any warmth, too.

The absence of emotion on both sides was concerning.

He'd expect that if one of them had true feelings for Elizabeth, they would have mentioned them.

And what had Luke meant about doing business? What sort of business was Luke involved in? David knew all the Amish shop owners by name and by face.

Luke Embers was not one of them.

Could he have some sort of business where he sold things elsewhere? Maybe. David knew Rachel Miller owned and operated a small restaurant in the downtown area of Green Lake, located outside the Amish community. Maybe Luke did the same.

When both men were gone, he resumed his walk around the property. Then, when he knew he couldn't avoid Elizabeth any longer, he headed back to the house.

Today he felt like an interloper, rather than a guest. David knew the change had come from within him, not Elizabeth.

Yet there wasn't anything he could do about it, other than to push through the discomfort. His work was what kept him on track. Without it, he felt lost.

Thankfully, tomorrow they could get back to doing actual work. Keeping busy would be a welcome relief, yet going to his workshop meant leaving the women alone, and he knew he couldn't do that. He sighed, stomped his feet to remove the worst of the snow, then stepped inside.

Hearing the murmur of voices coming from the second floor made him realize Elizabeth was still upstairs with her mother-in-law. After taking off his winter coat, hat and boots, he moved closer to the stairwell leading up to the second-story bedrooms, enjoying the sound of Elizabeth's voice.

He could listen to her sweet voice all day long, even if he didn't understand everything she was saying. The sense of peace that often eluded him fell softly around his shoulders.

Over dinner consisting of leftover soup

and boiled potatoes, he filled Elizabeth in on the brief interchange he'd overheard between Jacob and Luke.

Her brow furrowed in a frown. "*Ach*, while the interest in me is strange, the conversation sounds innocent enough."

David didn't necessarily agree. "What business was Luke talking about?"

"I'm not sure, maybe something to do with the wind-powered water pump that he and Adam created, it's been a popular addition among the Amish." She managed a smile. "I'm grateful for that, certain sure."

He nodded slowly, then thought about the fragment of conversation he'd overheard. "They issued no threat, that's true. But there was definite tension between them."

"As I read from the Bible to *Mammi* Ruth, I understood that I should look at the attention from Luke and Jacob differently. Focusing only on the negative side of things, rather than giving them the benefit of the doubt, isn't the right way. I would rather not think the worst of either man, *ja*?"

He frowned. "But their behavior was still strange, Elizabeth. Jacob warned Luke to stay away."

She sighed and nodded. "Mayhap there was

some disagreement between them on how to handle me, as Adam's widow." She managed a smile. "They likely seek to honor my deceased husband, despite me repeatedly telling them it's not necessary. I'm sure their attention will wane now that they are aware of my feelings."

David let it go. She could be right about Jacob and Luke. It occurred to him that the discussion between the two Amish men hadn't mentioned him as a potential threat to Elizabeth's favor. They didn't say anything about getting rid of David or trying to keep him from spending time with Elizabeth. They saw him as an *Englisch* outsider, and therefore not someone to be taken seriously. And they were probably right, as Bishop Bachman would want Elizabeth to marry someone within the community.

If she ever decided to remarry at all.

As much as he hated to admit it, he sensed the Amish men weren't responsible for setting his house on fire, and shooting at him.

The real culprit had to be someone close to Carson Wells. And his sole purpose was to extract revenge.

TEN

The following morning, Elizabeth was glad to find *Mammi* Ruth sitting at the side of her bed. "How are you feeling, today?"

"Sehr gut." The elder woman managed a smile. "I should like to come downstairs to break my fast."

Elizabeth managed to shake off the sliver of disappointment at not being able to share a private meal with David. *"Ach*, that's wonderful. Let's get you ready, *ja?"*

Fifteen minutes later, she escorted her mother-in-law down to the main level. David was already up and working at the stove.

"Good morning." He smiled warmly. "Breakfast should be ready soon."

"Denke, David." She couldn't seem to get used to how he jumped in to help. After getting *Mammi* Ruth settled at the table, she poured her a cup of coffee. "It's kind of David to cook, *ja?"*

Mammi Ruth glanced over at him, then frowned. "Women's work," she said curtly.

Apparently the kindness *Mammi* Ruth had felt toward David after he'd lifted her into bed had begun to wane.

David arched a brow but didn't say anything. Elizabeth wondered if he'd caught the gist of her mother-in-law's comment.

Elizabeth said grace, first in Pennsylvania Dutch for *Mammi* Ruth's sake, then again in English. "Lord, we humbly ask You to bless this food, this home and the people who are staying here, amen."

"Amen," David echoed.

The conversation was somewhat hampered by *Mammi* Ruth's lack of English and David's inability to understand Pennsylvania Dutch, but David didn't seem to mind. When they finished eating, she assisted Ruth back upstairs to rest.

When she returned, she found David doing the dishes.

"I can take care of this," she protested.

"So can I," he said with a grin. "*Mammi* Ruth seems a bit better. You really think she'll be okay by Wednesday when the Amish Shoppe reopens for business?"

"I hope so." She began drying the dishes. "It's a short week with the holiday, ain't so?"

"True." He hesitated, then added, "Speaking of the Amish Shoppe, I need to get some work done on the baby cradle that was struck by a bullet. Would you be willing to come with me? You could do some sewing while I work."

She hesitated, glancing toward the stairs leading to *Mammi* Ruth's room. "I should stay here in case she needs me."

David slowly nodded. "Of course, I understand. I'll stay then, too."

"You shouldn't have to give up your work for me," she protested.

"I'm not leaving you alone." There was an underlying note of steel in his tone. "I didn't imagine someone outside peering into the house in the middle of the night. If I thought I could lure the intruder away, I would."

"No, please, don't do that." She detested the idea of David putting himself in harm's way. "Certain sure it's better for us to stay together, *ja*?" Then another thought struck. "You could bring the cradle and the tools you may need here. Adam had been renovating one of the bedrooms upstairs. It's still a mess, but you are welcome to use that space."

If the barn had a woodstove, she'd offer that for him, but it was too cold to be of use over the winter months.

"Thank you for the offer. I wouldn't mind using the room but carrying the cradle back on foot would be difficult."

"We could walk to the Amish Shoppe together and use the phone there to call Liam. I'm sure he'd help drive us back with the cradle." She impulsively reached over to take his hand. "Please, David, I'd feel so much better if I wasn't causing you to get behind on your work."

He hesitated, then nodded. "That would be great, thank you."

"Wonderful." She breathed a sigh of relief. "*Mammi* Ruth should be okay for a short while, *ja?*"

"I would think so." A frown furrowed his brow. "I believe that whoever peered through the window was looking for me."

After the way someone had shot at him outside the Green Lake Grill, she was forced to agree. If that was true, though, why had the person peering through the window just left? Why not shoot at David through the glass?

She didn't have an answer. Thinking of the noon meal, she checked the pantry. Many staples were running low, which meant she'd need to ask some of the other women for assistance.

Leah's mother, Mary Moore, was very good

about offering to help. Elizabeth had grown closer to the Moore family after Leah had been injured by a man who'd mistaken Leah for Shauna. She decided they should take a small detour to Leah's family farm before heading to the Amish Shoppe. David agreed.

Mary Moore promised to stop by to check on *Mammi* Ruth, while bringing additional eggs, canned fruits and vegetables and chicken. Elizabeth paid her with money she'd earned from selling quilts.

As she walked beside David, she glanced at his profile. He was a few years older than Adam had been, yet she found him more appealing to the eye.

And in many other ways, too.

"Let's be careful along this stretch of highway." David put out a warning arm, tucking her close to his side as they approached the area where they'd been targeted by gunfire. "Stay here, closer to the trees."

He'd positioned himself so that he would take the brunt of an attack. But thankfully, there was no gunfire, or any other evidence that they had been followed.

Soon, the large red barn came into view, and she couldn't help but notice how desolate it looked on a day when there were no customers in attendance. It made her a little sad to realize that David often stayed in his workroom alone on the days the shops weren't open.

"Wait." David's steps slowed, and he put out his arm to prevent her from going any closer.

"What is it?" She whispered, even though there was no one around to overhear.

"I thought I saw someone moving around to the back of the barn." David frowned as he glanced around, seeing no one else nearby. "Liam promised to have a deputy swing by to keep an eye on the place."

It wasn't until that moment that she realized what he was feared. "Do you think the same person that set fire to your house might strike here?"

"Yes, that's exactly what I'm worried about," David admitted. "For once I wish I had a car."

"Or a horse and buggy," she said with a frown. They were out in the open, standing alongside the highway, mere yards from the Amish Shoppe parking lot. "*Ach*, I'm not sure what we should do. Stay or head back?"

David didn't answer for a long moment. "We'll stay, but we're going to run to reach the front doors before anyone can come around to see us, okay?"

She nodded and took the hand he offered,

praying her knee wouldn't cause her to be too slow. She gathered her dress with one hand. A moment later they were running as fast as possible toward the front doors of the Amish Shoppe, as if a bobcat was nipping at their heels.

David had never regretted giving up his previous life to lead the plain life of the Amish, until now.

He desperately wished for a car, or a phone that wasn't tucked away inside his workroom.

As he jammed his key into the lock, he saw a flash of red and blue lights from the corner of his eye. Still, he continued unlocking the door. He opened it and gently pushed Elizabeth inside.

"Are you okay?" he asked with concern.

Breathless, she nodded.

He glanced around the interior but didn't see anyone nearby. He patted her arm. "Stay here for a moment. I'm going to check in with Liam's deputy."

Clutching her cloak close, she blew out a breath. "Okay."

He slipped back outside and lightly jogged to the squad. Recognizing Garrett Nichol, Liam's chief deputy, he reached for the passenger-side door handle. He opened the door so they could talk. "I need you to check around back. I saw someone disappear around the building as Elizabeth and I walked up."

Garrett frowned and got out. "I'll go. You should wait for me."

"No, I'm coming with you." David closed the door and quickly joined Garrett. There were tracks in the snow, proof that he hadn't imagined the guy.

Garrett led the way, gun in hand. But after they turned the corner, there was no one hiding back there.

David frowned, then noticed a set of footprints heading toward the woods. The footprints were widely spaced, as if the guy had been running. The same way he and Elizabeth had run to reach the safety of the building. "He went that way."

"I really need you to stay back," Garrett said firmly. "Remember what happened at the Green Lake Grill? We know this guy is armed and doesn't hesitate to shoot. I want you to stay put. I'll check in with you later, okay?"

Difficult to argue, so he reluctantly nodded. As Garrett headed toward the woods, David hurried back to Elizabeth, silently praying for the deputy's safety.

"What did you find?" She searched his gaze.

"Footprints heading into the woods. I think he's long gone, but stay close, anyway." He took her arm as they walked quickly toward the back of the barn, where their shops were located.

"Did you ask Garrett for a ride back?" Elizabeth stayed close as he unlocked his showroom.

"No, but he'll return to check in. And I can use the phone to call Liam if needed." He glanced at her. "Do you regret coming along?"

"*Ach*, no. 'Tis better we were together than for you to have been alone, *ja*? Although I can't say my boots are made for running," she added wryly.

It bothered him that she'd been forced to run for her life. "The good news is that we'll get a ride back to your house, which should help." David pulled his damaged cradle toward the front door and then grabbed the hand tools and sandpaper he would need to finish the project. He packed the tools inside a burlap bag.

He couldn't help wondering what Garrett had found. He was feeling guilty over allowing the deputy to go alone, but then heard a knock on his rear workshop door.

Hurrying over, he opened the door just a

crack to make sure Garrett was the one standing there. When he saw the deputy, he opened the door wider and gestured for him to come inside.

"Find anything?" David asked hopefully as Elizabeth joined them.

"No, but I'm glad you and Elizabeth arrived when you did. Your arrival likely scared him off." Garrett's expression was grim. "Although I have to ask, why are you here?"

"It's my fault." David sighed. "I wanted to work on finishing my baby cradle that had been damaged by gunfire but didn't want to leave Elizabeth home alone. I was awakened by noises from someone peeking in through one of the windows last night, and remain worried about her safety."

Garrett grimaced. "That's not good. And you couldn't call Liam because you didn't have a phone."

"Exactly." David shrugged. "I didn't find anyone lurking nearby and all was quiet last night. Maybe I'm just being paranoid."

"I think it's obvious the shooter from the Green Lake Grill wants you injured or dead. Between the gunfire and your house burning to the ground, he isn't being very subtle," Garrett pointed out. He turned to look around the workroom. "I'm happy to offer you a ride back to Elizabeth's. How much of this stuff do you want to take?"

"A ride would be great." He hesitated, wishing he could take more, but Garrett's squad car wasn't that large. "Just the baby cradle and my bag of tools is fine."

"Okay, let's hit the road. I'll feel better once you're back at the house." Garrett gestured for them to lead the way through the back room to the showroom.

David carried the cradle while Garrett grabbed his bag of tools. Elizabeth took care of locking his showroom doors as well as the main doors on their way out.

Garrett opened the trunk of his car for David, then set the bag on the floor in the back seat. Soon they were settled inside and heading back toward the Amish community.

"You'll tell Liam what happened?" David asked as Garrett pulled up in front of Elizabeth's house. "I'm very concerned about the safety of the Amish Shoppe."

"We're keeping an eye on the place." Garrett met his gaze in the rearview mirror. David nodded, remembering the cameras Liam had put up.

"What about the cameras?" Elizabeth asked

as if reading his mind. "They'll provide information, *ja*?"

"I—uh, yeah." Garrett looked surprised that she knew about them. "I've already asked Liam to check the video. Hopefully we'll get a good look at the guy's facial features."

"Unless he's wearing the black ski mask again," David muttered.

"There is that." Garrett looked grim as he pulled over to park in front of Elizabeth's house.

"Will you ask Liam to come see me when he has a chance?" David pushed open his door. "I'd like to know if he learned anything from the Green Lake Grill shooting incident."

"There's been nothing new that I'm aware of." Garrett shut down the engine. "But sure, I'll ask him to swing by."

"*Denke*, Garrett, the ride was very much appreciated." Elizabeth offered a wan smile as she slid out of the car. "Take care."

"You, too." There was concern in Garrett's gaze as he carried the bag of tools up to the house. He hesitated before leaving. "David, I really wish you'd have brought the cell phone with you."

"There's no electricity to keep it charged," David reminded him.

"God will protect us," Elizabeth added.

A look of frustration crossed Garrett's face, but he nodded before returning to the squad car and driving away.

David carried the cradle up the narrow staircase and found the spare room Elizabeth had mentioned. She'd indicated Adam had been renovating the room, but as a carpenter, he couldn't quite understand what vision her deceased husband had for the space.

There were tools lying around, and several boards propped up against the wall. Elizabeth set the burlap bag on the floor, then looked around with a grimace.

"It looks rougher than I remembered," she admitted. "Mayhap I should ask Luke to finish the project."

"Luke is a carpenter?"

"No, but I'm sure he knows enough about woodworking, ain't so? And Adam may have told him what he had planned for this space."

Everything inside him rejected that idea. "I'd rather do the work myself," David quickly offered. "Besides, what difference does it make what Adam wanted? This room is yours now, to use as you wish." He eyed the dimensions, gauging the space. "There's good morning light from those windows facing east. You may want to use this as a sewing room."

"A sewing room?" Her light brown eyes brightened with excitement. "*Sehr gut*, that would be wonderful." Then her face fell. "But I can't ask you to do the work for free."

"You didn't ask, I offered. And I'd like to do this for you. After all, you've been feeding me for the past few days. It's the least I can do in return."

"Happy to do so, *ja*?" She smiled. "I would like that sewing room very much. But you must promise me your furniture will come first."

He'd rather her renovations took priority, then again, he'd need to increase his stock over the winter months if he was to rebuild his house come spring. The amount of work facing him was staggering, but he reminded himself that God would guide him. "I'll find a way to do both," he assured her.

After she left, he glanced around the room again, anxious to get to work. The idea of helping Elizabeth in this way made him happy. It had been two years since he did this type of home construction, but he looked forward to the challenge.

In the back of his mind, though, he thought it was a shame the room wouldn't be used as a nursery.

He was curious about the fact that Elizabeth and Adam didn't have children. Not that their relationship was any of his business. Still, it was the natural order of things.

Was the lack of children one of the reasons Elizabeth did not want to marry?

He couldn't think of a way to ask that wouldn't come across as rude.

After pulling out his tools, he arranged the workspace to his liking. As always, working with wood was soothing. After he replaced the damaged section of the cradle, he began sanding the wood until it was flawlessly smooth to the touch.

He had to roll up his shirtsleeves as he worked. When Elizabeth called him for the noon meal, he was surprised to realize he'd been working for several hours without a break.

The cradle was coming along nicely. By tomorrow he should be able to begin applying the shellac.

"David?" Elizabeth called again.

"Coming." He glanced around the room once more, noticing the closet tucked in the corner. Curious, he went over to look inside, only to find the door was locked.

Strange. Why lock a closet door? There was no sign of a key, either.

He hurried downstairs, to the wonderful scent of chicken soup. "Smells amazing."

"I hope you like it."

"I will. Do you know what's in the closet in that spare room?"

"No, why do you ask?"

"It's locked."

"Locked?" She turned to face him, her expression guarded. "Why would it be locked?"

A shiver of apprehension slid down his spine. "I was hoping you could tell me. There must be some reason Adam had decided to lock the door."

Her face turned grim and she stared down at the floor for a moment, before finally meeting his gaze. "Only to keep me away, certain sure."

"What? Why?"

"*Ach*, I have no idea, as Adam didn't choose to enlighten me before he died." She picked up the tray. "Excuse me, I must take this to *Mammi* Ruth." Without saying anything more, she hurried from the room.

David was shocked by her response, even as he realized once again how strained the relationship had been between Elizabeth and her husband.

It also explained why she'd been so upset that he'd gone to the Green Lake Grill without including her in his plans. It seemed Adam had done the same.

Yet he couldn't help but wonder what sort of secrets a husband would keep from his wife?

In his mind? Nothing good.

ELEVEN

After getting *Mammi* Ruth settled with her tray, Elizabeth left, glancing for a moment at the spare room as she walked by. It was strange the closet door was locked. Deep down, she was angry with Adam for doing such a thing. Mayhap she should have noticed, but in truth she hadn't bothered to become involved with what he was doing.

She felt her cheeks heat with shame as she realized how she didn't know Adam at all. Her fault, for not doing more.

Although he certainly hadn't supported her selling her quilts at the Amish Shoppe, either.

Yet it was clear now that two people doing the wrong thing had aggravated the tension between them. Her shoulders slumped as a wave of regret hit hard. She needed to take responsibility for the role she'd played in the gulf between them. No matter what she'd thought at the time, her actions were not much better than Adam's. Returning to the kitchen, she caught David's apologetic gaze.

"I'm sorry if I made you upset," he murmured. "That wasn't my intent."

"*Ach*, you didn't. It's no secret that Adam and I weren't close, *ja*?" She filled two plates and brought them to the table. Reaching for David's hand, she managed a smile. "We still have much to be thankful for."

"Yes, we do. Dear Lord, we thank You for this wonderful food we are about to eat, and we ask that You continue to guide us on Your chosen path. Amen."

"Amen." She gently squeezed his hand, then released it. It was very telling that she felt closer to David when they said grace, compared to the meals she'd shared with Adam. Again, the fault was mostly hers, as she knew she'd resented the arrangement.

"Do you have a key to the closet?" David asked.

She frowned with annoyance. "No, but I can look for it. I gave away his clothing, of course, but there are odds and ends that I haven't bothered to look at too closely. I highly doubt there's anything of interest inside."

"You're probably right. It just seems odd the door would be locked."

"He may have been repairing a wall in there and locked the door by accident." She didn't want to talk about Adam. "The room is adequate for you to work in, *ja*?"

"Yes, it's fine," he assured her. "I appreciate you allowing me to do so. I know my woodworking causes a lot of dust."

"I don't mind." She focused on eating. The barn would have been better suited for his needs, and she wondered how difficult it would be to put a woodburning stove inside to warm the space.

Then realized she was being ridiculous. This arrangement with David was temporary. Not permanent. As soon as the danger was over, things between them would go back to normal.

Mayhap she would miss his generous help with the chores, and his company. She found herself wondering if she would have felt closer to Adam if they had been friends first, before Bishop Bachman had deemed they should marry.

Somehow, she didn't believe so. Only because Adam wasn't the sort of man she'd befriend under normal circumstances.

There hadn't been anything wrong with him, just that his nature was a bit abrasive. Not as much as Jacob's, but similar in some ways. Arrogant, authoritative, and very much steeped in the old ways. Well, except when it came to creating the wind-powered water pump, which had been one of his best ideas. And one she often thought he should have done more with.

Too late now.

She did her best to shake off her troubled thoughts. There was no sense in being upset with Adam, especially when he wasn't here to defend himself.

"Please don't be upset, Elizabeth." David lightly touched her hand. "I didn't mean to bring up painful memories."

"*Ach*, not painful just—confusing," she admitted. "It's not our place to question God's plan, but sometimes I find that difficult."

"Me, too," David agreed. "I guess that makes us human."

"*Ja.*" She blew out a breath, finished her meal, then smiled. "Certain sure we have much to do today, so we should get to work."

"Yes." David had already finished his meal, too, and again helped her with the dishes. Then he chopped more wood for the fire, before heading up to the second-floor bedroom to work on his cradle.

The hours passed by quickly, more so than

normal. She found the scent of sawdust pleasant, although *Mammi* Ruth complained about it.

"I'll clean up the dust when he's finished, *ja*?" She smiled and tucked the quilt around her. "I'll have David show you the cradle. It's very nice."

"I wish God had seen fit to bless you and Adam with children," *Mammi* Ruth said mournfully. "I would have liked to be a *grossmammi*."

Elizabeth didn't know what to say to that. Once she'd wanted babies, but when they didn't come, she was also a bit relieved. It had been a note of contention between them, Adam wanting her to be examined by the midwife to determine the problem.

She'd declined to do so, declaring they should put their trust in God's hands, instead.

"I'll be downstairs sewing if you need me, *ja*?" It was her habit to stay close to the wood-burning stove so she could keep it well stocked with wood.

Something she didn't need to worry about now that David was staying there.

Humbling to realize how much better things seemed now that David was living with them. Not just the feeling of being safe, but the sheer enjoyment of sharing meals, talking, and working side by side on routine chores.

Mayhap she was wrong to avoid marriage.

Mayhap she only needed the right man to share her life.

By the time dinnertime rolled around, David was satisfied with his progress on the cradle. The repair looked seamless; no one would ever know that it had been marred by a bullet.

After he stained the wood with a soft cloth, the hue of the wood shone through.

Now there was nothing more he could do until the stain soaked in and dried. If he were at his workshop, he'd choose another project to work on.

But he'd only brought the cradle to Elizabeth's. The spare room space was nice, especially after he'd stored all of Adam's tools on one side, near the closet, but it wasn't big enough for his larger projects, like the grandfather clock he was working on, and the large dresser that matched the four-post headboard he'd recently completed. He remembered there hadn't been a headboard in *Mammi* Ruth's room, and considered making her one.

The other bonus for the day was that there

had been no interruptions from the intruder. He hoped that meant they'd given up.

As Elizabeth was preparing a tray for *Mammi* Ruth, he heard a car engine. Peering warily through the window, he relaxed when he recognized Liam's SUV.

"Come in," David said, opening the front door for the sheriff. "Do you have news?"

Liam glanced around for Elizabeth.

"She's upstairs with her mother-in-law," David told him. "Do you want her to be here?"

"No, that's not necessary." Liam eyed him thoughtfully. "I don't know how much she knows of your past."

"She knows everything." He could tell something wasn't quite right. "Tell me, Liam. What did you find out?"

"Carson Wells has a younger brother, Bryon Wells. Apparently, he's been pretty vocal about how much he hates and blames you for killing Carson. Carson's father, Marvin, has also been spouting off his mouth."

The news wasn't much of a surprise. "Do you know if Bryon is here in Green Lake?"

"No sign of him yet." Liam shrugged. "We're keeping an eye out but you know from experience that the rich often hire others to do their dirty work."

Liam was talking about the events from two months ago, when David and Shauna had been kidnapped at gunpoint. "I do, yes."

"Anyway, we're keeping an eye on the Amish Shoppe and checking in at the Green Lake Grill. The man you saw outside earlier today was wearing a ski mask, so we couldn't identify him. Hopefully we'll find something more to go on, soon."

"Thank you, Liam." David knew Liam's duties as sheriff kept him busy, and appreciated that he'd come all this way to update him. "I guess we know Bryon is likely responsible for the shootings and setting the fire."

"Maybe, but don't forget our witness saw an Amish man standing near your place before the fire." Liam shrugged. "I'm still keeping an open mind."

"I overheard Luke and Jacob discussing Elizabeth." David went on to fill Liam in on the entire conversation. "They didn't mention me at all, so I don't think they view me as a threat."

"Hmm, that is interesting." Liam glanced over to where Elizabeth was coming down the stairs. "Hi, cousin, how are you doing?"

"*Sehr gut*, Liam." Elizabeth gestured to the kitchen. "Would you like to join us for dinner? There's plenty of chicken soup and bread to go around."

"No, thanks, Shauna is waiting for me." The goofy grin on Liam's face made David smile. The sheriff and David's niece were madly in love, and David was grateful that they'd found each other. "I wanted to check in with you earlier, but had to cover one of my deputies that got sick. In addition to the man you saw earlier today, Garrett mentioned you saw someone looking in the window?"

David nodded. "I believe so, yes. Although it could have been innocent enough."

"The Johannesburg boys are known to get into mischief," Elizabeth said. "Mayhap they are responsible for the footprints near the window."

"Are they old enough to have shoved you to the ground and to hit me over the head?" David asked.

She hesitated. "They could have pushed me down, but I don't think they would hit you over the head. Benjamin, the eldest, is only twelve."

"Hmm. Either way, I'd like both of you to remain alert to any potential trouble," Liam said. "I'm glad things have been quiet so far."

"*Denke*, Liam. I'm safe with David and God watching over me, *ja*?"

"I'm glad." Liam held David's gaze for a long moment. "Do you have a gun? Or a knife?"

"No, and I don't want one." He raised a hand in protest. The memory of how he'd killed Carson Wells with just his fist lingered in his mind. "We'll be fine."

Liam hesitated, as if he wanted to say something more, then nodded. "I'm only concerned because you're rather isolated out here. Your closest neighbor is one of your suspects."

David couldn't argue because Liam was right. They were isolated. Yet he wasn't going to carry a gun or a knife, no matter what. "I know."

"God will protect us," Elizabeth said.

"I know He will. Take care." Liam turned away and left. David closed the door behind him.

"I should have asked how you felt about me carrying a weapon." He met Elizabeth's gaze. "Would you feel safer if I did? After all, Carson Wells' brother, Bryon, is angry with me, not you. If he is the one responsible, my being here puts you in danger. I wouldn't want you hurt because of me."

"No, David. Certain sure, I understand your reluctance to do so." Her smile was gentle. "*Komm*, we should eat our dinner, *ja*?"

He nodded and followed her to the kitchen. They'd barely finished eating when *Mammi* Ruth called from her room.

"Go ahead, I'll start the dishes." David didn't mind helping Elizabeth with the kitchen chores. And maybe it was his imagination, but *Mammi* Ruth didn't seem quite as cranky as usual.

When the chores were finished, he headed outside again to walk the property. This time, he paid extra attention to the footprints in the snow.

He inspected the ones near the window again, then followed the path across the yard. Not surprising, he found a set of prints leading toward Jacob's property.

Normally he wouldn't trespass, but tonight he didn't hesitate. He crossed into Jacob's yard and continued following the prints all the way to the barn.

Not the house, though. Which made it difficult to know if Jacob had been the one to take the path or if someone else had? The uncertainty bothered him. He did not want to accuse someone of an action if they were in fact innocent.

And he remembered how Jacob had denied pushing Elizabeth to the ground. At the time, he'd thought the Amish man's surprise looked genuine.

But if that was the case, why had he continued to pursue Elizabeth? Was it truly a matter of wanting to expand his farm by using her land?

Hard to say, since he knew of several Amish who shared farm fields. If Jacob asked to use some of Elizabeth's land, she'd likely agree.

Shaking his head in frustration, David turned to head back to Elizabeth's. Movement past a window in Jacob's house caught his eye, and he felt certain the man had seen David walking around.

Why hadn't Jacob come out to confront him? Was it possible the Amish man knew David suspected him of wrongdoing?

By the time he'd finished walking the property, he was feeling chilled. He took a moment to stack the recently chopped wood in his arms, before heading inside.

Elizabeth was sitting in a chair close to the fire, sewing. She glanced up when she saw him. "*Ach*, I was beginning to worry something had happened to you."

"I'm fine." He didn't go into detail about the prints leading to Jacob's house. "The temperature is dropping a bit, though."

"I'm always happy to have a white Christmas."

"Me, too." He fed more wood into the stove, then closed the hatch. "Do you have any special Christmas traditions?"

"Not particularly. We don't make a big deal out of exchanging gifts, the way the *Englisch* do. But we often have a celebratory gathering at one of the neighbors' homes."

He nodded. There had not been much money while he was growing up, so gifts were scarce then, too. He thought about the wooden quilt rack he'd hidden in his workshop.

Would she accept such a gift from him? He didn't think it was too personal, yet he also didn't want her to feel obligated to reciprocate in kind.

"Good night, David." Elizabeth had rolled her fabric pieces together and stored them in a bag. "I'll see you in the morning."

"Good night." He waited for her to head upstairs before washing up and stretching out on the sofa. After being up half the night and working all day, he was physically exhausted.

He fell asleep almost instantly. But it didn't take long for dreams of the night he'd punched Carson Wells to grab on to him.

The moment Carson flew backward beneath

his punch, his head hitting with a loud thud against the corner of the bar... He sat bolt upright on the sofa, his pulse pounding as he struggled to breathe.

A nightmare. It was just a nightmare.

Or was it? Had he imagined the thudding sound?

He tossed the quilt aside and stood. In the darkness, he peered out the window where he thought someone had been watching last night.

There was no one out there that he could see, but then his gaze snagged on the blue cellar doors. One of them was slightly higher than the other.

And they hadn't been that way earlier when he'd walked the property.

"David? Did you hear that?"

He turned to see Elizabeth coming toward him down the stairs. She clutched a shawl around her shoulders, and her expression was anxious.

Not his imagination. "Yes, but I want you to stay here." He sat down and pulled on his boots. "I'll check it out."

"I'd rather go with you." Her gaze was full of fear. "Better for two of us, *ja*?"

"No." He winced at the sharpness of his tone. "Elizabeth, please wait here for me, okay?"

She reluctantly nodded.

He pulled on his jacket, once again grabbed a stick of firewood and headed outside. He quickly rounded the house and walked straight to the cellar doors.

They were still ajar, and he felt certain the thudding noise was from someone dropping one of them.

"Hello?" he called loudly. "Who's there?"

No response.

He glanced around, but there were too many footprints now to ascertain if some were fresh or left by him earlier.

"Is anyone down there?" He waited a moment before bending over to lift the cellar door open.

A series of wooden steps disappeared in the darkness. He should have brought a lantern.

As if hearing his thoughts, Elizabeth came over to stand beside him, lantern in hand. "I saw you open the cellar door," she whispered. "You think someone is down there?"

"It's possible." He took the lantern. "Go back inside."

"No, David. I intend to stay with you." She gripped the back of his coat with her hand.

There wasn't time to argue. He carefully descended the stairs, using the lantern to illuminate the area.

The cellar wasn't overly large and held the typical food items one would expect. Several canned goods and cured meats. When he reached the bottom, he swept the light in a complete circle, but no one was there.

His gaze landed on puddles of water on the floor. He frowned, bending down to examine them more closely. They were spaced about shoulder length apart and reminded him of the damp spots he'd found inside the Amish Shoppe after chasing off the intruder.

"Someone was here," Elizabeth whispered.

"Yes." He slowly straightened and once again swept the lantern over the area. There were no potential hiding spaces that he could see. He crossed over to peer closer at the shelves. They were basic and sturdy; the canned goods she stored here were lined up in neat rows. "Do you see anything out of place?"

"No, but I don't keep a detailed inventory of my goods, either," she admitted. "Certain sure others are welcome to borrow what they might need, but it's very strange to do so in the middle of the night, *ja*?"

"Yeah." He didn't like it, but he turned back toward the stairs.

Without warning, the cellar door slammed shut. He lunged up the stairs to stop it, but too late.

He pushed against the door, expecting it to open, but it didn't move.

Panic gripped him by the throat. He pushed again, using all his strength. The door moved just a fraction of an inch, but no further. He tried again, a third time, with the same result.

The wind hadn't closed the cellar doors, but someone had.

They were trapped!

TWELVE

Watching David struggle with the cellar door sent a warning chill down her spine. "Why won't it open?"

"I don't know." He remained on the steps, using his hands to feel along the edge of the door.

The cellar was cold, not as bad as being out in the elements, but not warm enough for them to spend the night in, either. She shivered, and tried not to panic.

Lord, help us escape!

"I should have taken Liam's offer of a knife," David muttered harshly. He glanced at her over his shoulder. "Do you have anything down here that we can use to saw through the wood?"

"I don't think so." She went over to examine the shelves. "I could break a jar if you think the sharp edge of a glass might help."

"Don't do that yet." David pushed hard

against the door again. She stepped closer, wondering if she could add her strength to the task.

David shoved at the door again. "It moves a little more each time. It's not locked… I think someone set something heavy on top."

"*Ach*, who would do such a thing?" Jacob? Luke? Or the brother of Carson Wells?

David didn't answer. He was breathing hard between forceful thrusts against the door.

She shivered again and clutched her cloak tight as the December chill seeped into her bones. How long would it take for them to become hypothermic? It wasn't as cold down here as it was outside, but it was far too chilled to sustain them for long. She didn't fear death, knowing she would be with God, but this wasn't how she expected to go.

And she couldn't help feeling a bit of regret at how she'd kept David at arm's length.

"It's moving," David said excitedly. "I think whatever was placed over the doors is slipping off."

"Like what?" She couldn't imagine what had been used to hold the doors down.

"I'm not sure." David sounded breathless.

"Can I help? Maybe with both of us pushing against it, we can move them farther?"

"I thought of that, but there isn't enough room for both of us on the stairs." He flashed a smile. "Don't worry, I won't stop until we get out of here."

She believed him. More than she'd ever believed anyone else. Clutching her cloak closer, she stamped her feet to stay warm. They would not die here tonight, but that didn't mean they were getting out soon.

She swallowed hard. What if *Mammi* Ruth needed her? What if the same person who locked them in had gone inside the house?

The thought reminded her of Adam's plan to add an interior staircase to the cellar so that there would be a passageway to go into the cellar from the kitchen. She hadn't seen the need, but now she desperately wished he had finished that project.

"Oomph." David grunted as he shoved against the door again. Her pulse kicked up as she saw the gap between the doors widen.

He was going to do it. David was going to get them free!

She prayed for God to give David the strength he needed. It was difficult to stand there doing nothing but feeling helpless. She glanced around the interior of the cellar again, trying to understand why anyone had come down here in the first place.

Lifting the lantern, she double-checked that she hadn't missed anything. The wooden shelves were long, the canned goods neatly placed.

It didn't make any sense.

"I think—I've got it." David groaned again, then the cellar door abruptly opened. It happened so fast he lost his footing. She lunged forward to break his fall.

He caught himself in time. Again, a smile creased his features. "Thanks. Let's get out of here."

He didn't need to ask twice.

"I'll go first." He mounted the stairs, taking a moment to peer over the edge of the cellar doors to look around. He must not have seen anything suspicious, because he climbed all the way out.

"It's clear. Hurry," he urged.

She quickly moved toward the steps. Going up while holding the lantern was awkward, but David lowered his hand to help. Soon she was standing outside the cellar, breathing the crisp cold air.

Then her gaze landed on the rusty metal

plow that had been set over the cellar doors. It took a moment for her to realize it was Jacob's.

"I know, it's very suspicious," David said, reading her thoughts. "But keep in mind anyone could have done this. Let's get inside."

He took the lantern, then clasped her hand. Together they rounded the corner of the house, then headed to the front door. David once again went first, sweeping the lantern around the interior of the living room before going all the way inside.

The warmth of the room washed over her. David set down the lantern, then continued searching the house, going all the way upstairs to make sure no one was hiding inside.

When he returned to the living room, his expression was grim. "There are damp prints in the room upstairs."

She sucked in a harsh breath. "Someone was here?"

"Whoever did this is gone now." David took a moment to add more wood to the stove. "I have to believe my efforts to break free of the cellar cut his time short."

"Oh, David." She crossed over to wrap her arms around his waist. Despite everything that had happened, she was grateful for his enduring strength and support. "*Denke* for getting us out of there."

He held her close for a long moment, as if needing the reassurance that they were fine, as much as she did. She buried her head against his chest for a moment, then pulled back just enough to look up at him.

A wave of longing caught her off guard, and she impulsively went up on her tiptoes to kiss him. She'd intended to show gratitude, but the moment their lips touched, she knew their embrace was so much more.

His kiss was warm and sweet, then abruptly ended as he lifted his head. "I'm sorry, I didn't mean to take advantage of the situation."

"You didn't, but I did." She stared up at him for a long moment. "Good night, David. Sleep well."

She pulled away and headed upstairs, wondering how it was possible she could enjoy kissing David in a way she hadn't with Adam. Was this warm glow a result of their recently escaping a dire situation?

Or an indication of something more?

Wow. David could barely think after Elizabeth's kiss. He hadn't deserved it, but of course could think of nothing more than kissing her again.

He forced himself to move, swallowing a groan as his muscles ached in protest. He'd never played football, but after slamming his hands against the cellar door for fifteen minutes straight, he had sympathy for those who had.

Thinking about the rusty plow weighing down the cellar door, he stumbled toward the sofa. The intruder hadn't locked the doors with a padlock, but the heavy plow had been somewhat effective at keeping them trapped long enough for the intruder to get inside the house.

But why? The obvious answer was to look for something. Yet there was no reason for Bryon Wells to do such a thing. Especially since the guy had taken several shots at him and had likely set his house on fire.

If Wells had been here, he could have easily fired down upon them in the cellar. It wasn't as if he and Elizabeth would have been able to escape.

He thought of the Amish man who'd been seen near his house before the fire had been set.

An Amish man that could have easily lugged the rusty plow over to the cellar door to trap them inside.

Was there a connection between the Amish and the *Englisch*? If so, he was missing it.

He pulled off his boots and stretched out on the sofa. The multiple incidents that had transpired over the past few days whirled like snowflakes in his mind, but the physical exertion of getting them out of the cellar eventually lured him to sleep.

After what seemed like a few minutes later, the sounds of movement from upstairs woke him. But when he looked outside, he could see dawn brightening the horizon.

Wincing a bit, he rose and padded across the room to feed the woodburning stove. He made a mental note to chop more wood later, if he could manage to raise his arms high enough to swing the ax. He rubbed his shoulders for a moment, then turned to see Elizabeth coming down the stairs.

"Good morning." Just seeing her made him smile. "I'm sorry I didn't have a chance to start breakfast."

"*Ach*, that's not a problem. I'm happy to do so." Her cheeks were pink, either from the heat or from the memory of their kiss.

He hoped it was the latter.

"I was thinking we should talk to Jacob today." Elizabeth brushed past him to gather the makings for breakfast. "We need to understand how his rusty plow came to be lying across the cellar doors, *ja*?"

He hesitated, then nodded slowly. The Amish way was to handle grievances between them without outside help, so it made sense to speak to Jacob directly. But he wanted to shield her from any potential disagreement. "I would be happy to talk to him. No need for you to come along."

She frowned. "I was trapped in the cellar, too, David."

"I know." It was his need to keep her safe that had given him the strength to push the heavy plow off the doors. "But I think this conversation should be between the two of us."

"I insist on going with you." There was a steely note of determination in her tone. "Jacob is my neighbor and therefore his actions are my concern, ain't so?"

Most of the time he admired her independence, but not today. He didn't think Jacob would speak freely in front of Elizabeth, but maybe that wasn't the worst thing.

Once they'd confronted him, Jacob would know without any doubt they were on to him. David would make it clear these incidents had to stop.

"Don't try to talk me out of it." Elizabeth lifted her chin, staring him down.

"Fine. Have it your way. We'll go see Jacob together." He tried not to let his frustration show.

"Denke." Elizabeth cracked eggs into a bowl, but before she could continue preparing for their meal, *Mammi* Ruth called from upstairs.

Elizabeth dried her hands on a towel. "I must help her get up."

He nodded, waiting for her to head upstairs before stepping up to the kitchen counter. He quickly took over the task of making eggs as he considered their plans for the day.

It would be good to talk to Liam about the cellar incident, and he considered taking a walk back to the Amish Shoppe to borrow the cell phone. Maybe after they'd spoken to Jacob.

Today was Tuesday, which meant tomorrow the Amish Shoppe would open again. But only for two days, as the Christmas holiday was nearly upon them.

The police investigation was going far slower than he liked. If they didn't uncover something critical soon, he'd end up spending the holiday here with Elizabeth and her mother-in-law.

He wasn't sure he'd be welcome at whatever family gathering they might be invited to. It didn't matter, really—he'd spent the last several Christmas holidays alone.

This must be God's plan for him. To humble him after the way he'd taken Carson Wells's life.

Elizabeth returned with *Mammi* Ruth in tow. He nodded in greeting, glad to see the woman was moving around more.

Staying isolated in her room wasn't healthy, emotionally or physically.

Elizabeth said grace in both languages, then they ate. He noticed *Mammi* Ruth eyeing him curiously more than once. He patted his mouth with a napkin, thinking he had food on his face, then wondered if the elder woman had discovered he and Elizabeth had shared a kiss.

Was it written all over his face?

He wouldn't be surprised.

After they finished eating, *Mammi* Ruth insisted on sitting in the living room for a while. He was about to help Elizabeth with the dishes when there was a knock at the door.

Elizabeth glanced at him in concern as he crossed over to open it. He'd expected Liam or Garrett, but their visitor was Luke Embers.

"I'd like to speak to Elizabeth." Luke didn't

look surprised to see him, which meant the word was out among the Amish community that David was staying here.

"Come in," David invited.

Luke shook his head, peering over David's shoulder. Elizabeth came over to join them.

When it became clear Luke wanted to speak to her alone, he headed back to the kitchen. Elizabeth and Luke spoke in low voices for a few minutes, before Luke left as abruptly as he'd arrived.

Mammi Ruth said something in Pennsylvania Dutch that he didn't quite understand. Then it hit him.

"Luke asked to court you, didn't he?"

Elizabeth inclined her head. "*Ja*, but I politely refused."

"Did he say anything about the rusty plow sitting along the side of your house?" David asked.

She shook her head. "I doubt he saw it. His place is located down the road a stretch in the other direction. Besides, we'll talk to Jacob about that, as it came from his property, ain't so?"

Now that Luke had shown up here, he thought it might be prudent to talk to him, too. But maybe he could do that later. He glanced at *Mammi* Ruth. She was watching him like a hawk about to swoop down on a helpless chick. He imagined she would have preferred Elizabeth to accept Luke's courting, or Jacob's.

Anyone but him, an *Englisch* outsider.

Ignoring her wasn't easy and he felt the sudden need to escape. He reached for his coat and hat. "I'll bring in more firewood."

He went out to the woodpile, then lifted the ax. His biceps screamed and quivered, so he set it back down and spent his time gathering wood.

Being trapped in the cellar meant the danger was far from over. Leaving Elizabeth and *Mammi* Ruth alone wasn't an option.

After he made four trips, he figured there was enough wood to hold them for a while.

He returned inside and was surprised to find *Mammi* Ruth in the kitchen working alongside Elizabeth. It was the first time he'd seen her do such a thing.

The strained expression on Elizabeth's features indicated the woman had tried to convince Elizabeth to court Luke.

He escaped by heading up to the spare bedroom. There, he examined the baby cradle and wiped it down in preparation for another coat of stain.

When that was finished, he cleaned up and walked over to the closet. He tested the door handle again. It was still locked.

Then he knelt on the floor and looked closer at the door handle. There were no tiny scratches like the kind he'd seen in the Amish Shoppe's main door. Whoever had come up here last night hadn't attempted to pick the lock.

Because he'd run out of time? Or because he didn't have the proper tools?

The idea of two separate men coming after them wouldn't leave him alone. One Amish, one *Englisch*. A theory he wanted to discuss in more depth with Liam.

Finding a couple of small, skinny nails, he tried to pick the closet lock. Unfortunately, his efforts were futile, so he quickly gave up.

Standing back, he figured he could kick the door frame with his foot to open it by force. But he needed to discuss that with Elizabeth first. She might not appreciate that, especially if there was nothing in there worth breaking the door down.

"David?" Her voice drew him to the top of the stairs. "Liam is here."

"Good." He quickly went down to the main living room. A quick glance confirmed

Mammi Ruth wasn't around. Elizabeth must have helped her to her room without his hearing. "Liam, I'm glad to see you. Do you have information for us?"

Liam nodded slowly. "Elizabeth told me about the incident with the cellar last night. I'm glad you were able to escape."

He nodded. "It was a frightening experience and I wished I'd taken the knife you offered."

In response Liam pulled the pocketknife from his pocket. "Here, take it. The blade is small but sharp. It's better than nothing."

He glanced at Elizabeth, who nodded in agreement. "Can't hurt, *ja?*"

"Thanks." David took the knife.

"I have a photo array for you to look at," Liam said.

"You do?" For the first time in a while, he felt a surge of hope that Liam was getting close to arresting the man responsible. At least one of the men responsible. "Show me."

Liam took out a sheet of paper and handed it to him. Six faces stared up at him.

Elizabeth came over to see, too. For long moments neither of them spoke.

Finally, David was forced to shake his head. "I'm sorry, Liam, but I don't recognize any of these men. This one here," he said, tapping the man who appeared to have a thicker neck and wider shoulders compared to the others, "appears to be the same size as the man who shot at me in the Amish Shoppe and outside the Green Lake Grill."

"He doesn't look familiar otherwise?" Liam asked.

David frowned, then understanding dawned. "He looks a little like Carson Wells."

"His name is Bryon Wells. He's Carson's younger brother. We found a witness who put him at the Green Lake Grill back on Saturday night with a group of other guys." Liam shrugged. "We'll keep checking for more intel, but so far have come up empty-handed."

Logically, it made sense that Bryon was responsible for shooting at him and burning his house.

But the rest? No way. The methods didn't match. The incidents at Elizabeth's were more scare tactics than attempts to kill them.

"I believe there are two separate things going on," he said. "Bryon is out to seek revenge against me, but these strange incidents here at Elizabeth's haven't been nearly as lethal. Well, except for trapping us in the cellar. My thought is that an Amish person is responsible for what's happening here."

Elizabeth gasped. "You mean like Jacob or Luke?"

"Or someone else we haven't considered." He glanced at Liam, who nodded in agreement.

"But why?" Elizabeth asked.

He had no idea. But if they didn't figure it out soon, he was afraid the person would do something far worse than barricading them in the cellar.

THIRTEEN

David's theory of two different issues going on made sense, but Elizabeth wasn't sure where that left them. The incidents around her house didn't make sense.

"I wish I knew who trapped us in the cellar," David said, a frown furrowing his brow. "That could have been detrimental to both of us."

"Yes, I'm very glad you escaped," Liam agreed. "My goal is to find Bryon Wells. I would be willing to talk to Jacob and Luke, too, but I doubt they'll cooperate."

"They won't," David said. "But I plan to have a conversation with Jacob today."

"*We* have a plan to talk to Jacob, ain't so?" She pinned David with a narrow glare. They'd already had this discussion and she wasn't going to change her mind.

David grimaced and nodded. "Yes, we will.

However, I don't hold out much hope that Jacob will readily admit his role in this."

She wished now that she had asked Luke about the rusty plow that had found its way to her cellar door. But she'd been taken aback by his request to court her, and hadn't remembered anything else. A request *Mammi* Ruth had overheard and welcomed.

Who better to marry than Adam's cousin? That way, Elizabeth would remain part of the Walton family, even with Luke's last name being Embers.

The conversation David had overheard between Jacob and Luke had indicated Jacob didn't approve of Luke's desire to court her. Which could be related to the fact Jacob wanted to do the same.

What had struck her the most, though, was the lack of emotion on Luke's face as he'd made the offer.

As if he were doing so out of duty, rather than caring for her on a personal level.

"Elizabeth?" David's voice drew her from her troubled thoughts. "Are you willing to accept a ride to the Amish Shoppe with Liam? I'd like to return the cradle and pick up something else to work on for the rest of the day."

"*Ach*, that would be fine. Let me check on *Mammi* Ruth first, *ja*?"

"Take your time." Liam turned to David. "Are you sure you don't want me to go with you to talk to Jacob?"

"No, that will only put him off even more," David admitted.

Elizabeth made sure her mother-in-law was comfortable and let her know they'd be gone for about an hour.

"How long will the *Englischer* stay with us?" *Mammi* Ruth asked.

Elizabeth hesitated, trying to figure out a way to respond. She purposefully hadn't told the older woman about the danger. "Mayhap through the Christmas holiday. We'll see, *ja*?"

Mammi Ruth grabbed her hand. "Don't let the *Englischer* prevent you from courting Luke," she said with a frown. "Best you stay true to your Amish roots, *ja*?"

"I'm not interested in marrying again, whether that man is Luke, Jacob or David." As soon as the words left her mouth, she knew they weren't entirely true. David's kiss had been wonderful. Since their embrace, all she could think about was kissing him again, to see if the first time was nothing more than an aberration.

"You're too young to remain unmarried," *Mammi* Ruth scolded. "Your duty is to help the Amish community thrive, and that means bearing children, ain't so?"

She wasn't sure that God intended for her to have children. "Certain sure I'll keep that in mind," Elizabeth said, trying to get off the subject. "We will be back soon."

Mammi Ruth waved her hand with a look of impatience. "Bah, I'll be fine."

Elizabeth quickly made her escape. If only Luke hadn't shown up while *Mammi* Ruth was sitting in the living room, listening to their conversation. She wouldn't have a moment's peace now that her mother-in-law knew of Luke's intent.

She returned to the main living area and reached for her cloak. "Where is the cradle? Are you ready to go?"

"It's already in the SUV." David opened the front door for her. They headed toward Liam's personal SUV. Before sliding into the front passenger seat, she glanced over her shoulder toward Jacob's farm.

Smoke billowed from the chimney, indicating he was at home. She made a mental note to walk over to see him when they returned from the Amish Shoppe.

"You'll both return to work tomorrow, won't you?" Liam asked, glancing at her.

"*Ja*, but only for a few days. The shops will be closed Friday through the Christmas holiday."

"Hopefully we'll find Bryon Wells today." Liam shrugged. "Someone will see him. His picture has been disseminated to all deputies."

"But you can't just arrest him," David protested. "You don't have proof that he's done anything wrong."

"No proof, but that doesn't mean he isn't a person of interest in an ongoing attempted homicide and arson investigation," Liam pointed out. "His threats alone may be enough for a search warrant. If we can find a weapon, we'll have a good chance at matching the slugs we found."

Elizabeth marveled at the rules of the legal system the *Englisch* followed. If there was proof that Jacob or Luke were responsible for the incidents at her home, Bishop Bachman and the elders would likely request restitution and banish the offender from the community.

"You mentioned there was an Amish man inside the Green Lake Grill?" David asked.

"Yes. But the description was such that it could be anyone." Liam shot her an apologetic look. "I don't mean to be demeaning, but one of the reasons the Amish dress simply is so they don't stand out in a crowd, right?"

"Certain sure," she agreed. "I don't blame the *Englischers* for not seeing past the clothing to the person within."

"Ouch," Liam muttered. "That's putting me in my place."

"What about height or weight?" David persisted. "They must have noticed something."

"Too subjective. Remember that witness who saw an Amish man standing near your house before the fire?" Liam asked. "She was all of five feet two inches tall. To her, a tall man is anyone over five ten."

"Still, knowing if the guy was tall or short might help," David insisted.

Elizabeth turned in her seat to look at David. "You believe the man in the Green Lake Grill was Jacob."

"I do, yes." He met her gaze directly as if daring her to argue.

Liam pulled up in front of the Amish Shoppe. Rather than waiting in the car, he followed them inside. David carried the cradle and set it in the showroom.

"Why not take the phone?" Liam asked, when David brought out another partially finished project to place in his SUV. "The battery should last until tomorrow."

"I don't know if that's allowed." David looked at her. She hesitated, remembering the cellar incident. What if something like that happened again?

"It's fine with me, *ja*?" She forced a smile.

"Are you sure?" David searched her gaze. "I don't want to make you uncomfortable."

"Certain sure." She was already uncomfortable, but not because of the phone.

Her attempt to keep him at arm's length was failing, in a big way.

And she couldn't find the strength to care.

David tucked the cell phone in his pocket, then carried the small end table out to Liam's SUV. When the end table and the tools were stored in the back, he squelched a flash of guilt.

Among the things he'd brought were small tools that may be helpful in getting the closet door open. He hoped to try that first, leaving forcing it open with brute force as a last resort.

"That's strange," Elizabeth said as Liam approached her house. "Earlier, there was smoke from Jacob's chimney. Now it's gone."

"Where would Jacob go?" David asked.

He met Liam's gaze in the rearview mirror. "Maybe the Green Lake Grill."

"I'll swing by to check it out after I drop you off," Liam said.

David nodded. If not for Elizabeth, he'd insist on going with Liam. Yet he didn't want to expose her to danger, or leave *Mammi* Ruth home alone for long.

He needed to put his trust in Liam's police skills and in God.

After he'd carried his end table to the spare room, he turned to find Elizabeth standing there. "Let's go see if Jacob is home. Mayhap something is wrong, *ja*?"

He doubted that, but nodded. They donned their winter clothing and walked outside. They rounded the house, heading past the cellar doors. He abruptly stopped. "Where's the rusty plow?"

Elizabeth's eyes were wide with surprise. "I don't know."

He reached for her hand, and they continued walking toward Jacob's house. They went to the front door, but no one answered their knock. The door wasn't locked, so they went inside.

"I don't see anything amiss," Elizabeth whispered.

He didn't, either. It felt wrong to be in another man's home, so they left, and walked out toward the barn.

"There's the rusty plow." He gestured toward the fence. "Back where it belongs."

"*Ach*, and no sign of Jacob," Elizabeth said.

They checked the barn, then gave up and returned to Elizabeth's. David had a bad feeling about Jacob's absence and the way the rusty plow had been returned to its original spot.

Almost as if Jacob had tried to pretend the incident in the cellar had never happened.

He hoped Liam found Jacob and Bryon Wells at the Green Lake Grill.

Keeping a keen eye out for any danger, he escorted Elizabeth back inside. He was glad he'd brought the cell phone along, although he'd need to keep it hidden from *Mammi* Ruth.

"Do you need me to help with anything?" He tried not to glance toward the spare bedroom where his end table was waiting. "I can help prepare the noon meal,"

"*Ach*, no need. I have that ready to go." She waved at the stairs. "Get some work done, *ja*? I plan to sew for a bit, too."

He nodded and quickly headed up the stairs. The end table needed some fine-tuning, so he worked on that for a while. When he was finished with the design, he picked up the small tools he'd brought along and went to work on the closet door.

At first he thought he was making progress, but the door remained stubbornly locked. He sat back, realizing Elizabeth's theory of the closet door being locked by accident wasn't logical. For one thing, they didn't normally lock their doors. And really, the more he thought about the cellar incident, the more he believed the intruder had come up here to look for something of Adam's. It was the only explanation that made sense.

He glanced over at the crowbar he'd sneaked into the bag of tools, just for this purpose.

Breaking through the doorjamb would make enough of a racket to be heard all the way downstairs. He suppressed a sigh and decided to approach the topic with Elizabeth when they sat down to eat. She was sensitive when it came to discussing her deceased husband's secrets, and he understood to a point.

No one liked finding out how much they'd been lied to.

"David?" Elizabeth called his name from the bottom of the stairs. "*Komm*, it's time to eat."

He took a moment to wash the sawdust from his hands and face, before joining them. He inwardly groaned when he saw *Mammi* Ruth seated at the table.

No way to discuss breaking into the locked closet now. He forced himself to ignore her scowl as he sat beside Elizabeth.

Elizabeth said grace in both Pennsylvania Dutch and in English. The act of including him only seemed to annoy *Mammi* Ruth more.

The meal was delicious. He decided then and there to give Elizabeth the quilt rack he'd built for her. If she didn't want to accept it as a Christmas gift, he'd press her to see it as a thank-you for feeding him these past few days.

When they finished eating, *Mammi* Ruth said something he didn't understand. Elizabeth nodded and glanced at him. "She's not feeling well," she explained. "I'll take her back to her room."

It was his turn to be irked when he realized Elizabeth hadn't finished her meal. "I can do that for you," he offered.

"No, it's fine." She dabbed at her mouth, then rose to her feet. "*Komm, Mammi* Ruth."

The older woman stood and leaned on Elizabeth as they made their way upstairs. He finished eating, then took his dishes and *Mammi* Ruth's to the sink.

When Elizabeth returned, he joined her at

the table. "I'd like your permission to break into the locked closet."

A flash of concern darkened her eyes.

"I'll repair the damage," he quickly added. "I don't mind the work. I just think we should know what, if anything, Adam hid in there."

She finally nodded. "Of course, we should know what is inside, *ja*?" She didn't look happy about their prospects. "On one condition."

He eyed her warily. "Like what?"

She sighed. "We will not tell *Mammi* Ruth anything negative about her son. It wouldn't do any good. Certain sure she wouldn't believe us." Elizabeth paused, then added, "And if we find something that would tarnish Adam's reputation, we will not involve Liam." She arched a brow, likely expecting an argument. "I will either keep the information to myself, or Bishop Bachman and the elders will decide how to manage it, *ja*?"

He didn't like the idea of leaving the issue within the Amish community, but he nodded, understanding her need to protect Adam's memory. "I agree." He stood and moved to the sink. "We'll finish the dishes first."

Elizabeth was unusually quiet as they cleaned the kitchen. He could tell she was apprehensive about what they might find.

He led the way upstairs and picked up the crowbar. "Are you ready?"

She nodded. Slipping the flat edge of the crowbar beneath the trim around the door, he spread his feet and pulled. The wood came free without much force, clattering to the floor. He then pried the door open.

When he looked inside, though, he didn't see anything obvious. The closet appeared empty.

"Help me!"

Elizabeth whirled at the sound of *Mammi* Ruth's voice. "*Ach*, I hope she didn't fall again."

"Do you want me to come with you?" He made the offer, although he was anxious to examine the interior more closely.

"*Ja*, please." Elizabeth hurried over to the next room.

He leaned the crowbar up against the wall and quickly joined them. *Mammi* Ruth was once again lying on the floor and this time she was crying.

"Shh, *komm*, now, it's okay. You're going to be fine." Elizabeth looked up at him in concern. "I must get the doctor to see her."

He nodded. "Allow me to get her back to bed, okay?"

Elizabeth stepped aside to make room for him. His muscles were still achy and sore from breaking free of the cellar, but he ignored the discomfort.

"Ask her to put her hands around my neck," he instructed.

Elizabeth did so, and the woman complied. He lifted her off the floor and managed to take the two steps to reach the bed.

He did his best to ease her down onto the mattress.

"*Denke*, David," *Mammi* Ruth whispered. Lines of pain bracketed her mouth. She said something more, and this time, he understood that she was agreeing to see a doctor.

"I'll go now," Elizabeth promised.

He swallowed a protest, knowing that whatever was in the closet would keep. No reason to rush in and break down the door.

"Would you like me to come with you?" he asked. "I worry about you going alone."

"*Ach*, there is no need. I will be fine in the daytime. Shouldn't take me too long to fetch him, *ja*?"

"Then I'll stay here and keep an eye on *Mammi* Ruth."

"*Denke*." Elizabeth tucked the quilt around her mother-in-law's shoulders. She reassured the woman in her native language, before turning away.

He moved to give her room, his gaze going to the window. *Mammi* Ruth's room overlooked the barn and even from here, he could see the padlock he'd placed on the doors.

Then a plume of smoke rising from the far corner of the structure caught his eye. "Elizabeth?"

"*Ach*, what is it?" She joined him at the window, then sucked in a harsh breath. "A fire?"

He whirled and ran down the steps to the main level. He dragged on his coat as he barreled through the front door. His heart was beating so fast he could feel it pounding against his sternum.

The scent stung his nose, the smoke heavier here. When he rounded the barn, he let out an angry hiss as he saw the fire that had been started there. Worst of all, some of the wood he'd chopped had been used to create the blaze.

Just like the fire at his home, this was no accident.

He scooped up snow and tossed it on the flames. It helped, but not enough. He spun around to head back inside. They needed buckets of water to douse the fire.

If they didn't get it under control, Elizabeth could lose everything.

FOURTEEN

Fire! It wasn't Elizabeth's first exposure to fire. With so many woodburning stoves among the Amish, it had certainly happened before. But the source being her barn spurred her into action. She filled buckets of water, quickly handing them to David as he came inside.

"Will others come to help?" he asked on the third trip.

"*Ach*, they should." She continued filling buckets of water from the faucet in the sink, thankful for the wind-powered pump that allowed for indoor plumbing. "How bad is it?"

"Bad enough." David hurried back outside.

Through the kitchen window, she could see the swirling smoke rising toward the sky. From this angle, she couldn't see the fire, though, as it was located at the far corner of the barn.

Based on David's grim features, and knowing what had happened at his home, she knew the fire had been intentionally set. But for what purpose? That reasoning was out of her reach.

Soon Jacob and the Moore family came out to help. They, too, had brought buckets of water from their respective homes.

Would it be enough to douse the blaze?

She tried not to dwell on the possibility of the fire moving from the barn to the house. If the men couldn't get the barn fire under control soon, she'd need to stop filling buckets long enough to get *Mammi* Ruth outside.

Please, Lord, help us save the house!

Her arms grew sore from filling then carrying the water buckets to the door and back, but she didn't stop. She could tell David was just as exhausted going between the house and the barn lugging the water. She caught a glimpse of some of the men scooping up snow to use, as well.

"We're winning the battle," David said when he came back for more water. "Thanks to the help of your neighbors, we're close to dousing the fire."

"Sehr gut." She couldn't drum up a smile. The situation was still too precarious for her peace of mind.

The side portion of the barn collapsed in a resounding crash. Moments later, the rest of the barn fell, too. She stared in shock, her mind struggling to come to grips with the loss. The only reassurance she had was that she didn't see any yellow and orange flames.

David and the others continued dousing water on the barn. She understood that if they weren't careful the glowing embers could start up again.

When she feared her arms might fall right off her body, David returned. His face was blackened with soot, but he gave her a nod. "Take a break."

"Are you sure?" Her arms hung loose at her sides, pain radiating up to her neck. In truth, she wasn't sure she could continue hauling buckets of water, even if her life and *Mammi* Ruth's depended on it. "Is the fire out?"

"I believe so, and so do the others who probably have more experience than I do." He stared at her for a long moment. "You know this was no accident."

She sank down on the closest kitchen chair. "I know it's not. What have the others said?"

"We've been too focused on fighting the fire to talk about it in any detail," David admitted. "Yet I can tell by the way they've exchanged concerning glances that they believe it's suspicious."

As if on cue, Ezekiel Moore came inside. "*Ach*, Elizabeth, do you have any idea how this happened?"

"I don't." She glanced at David, who looked a little confused as Ezekiel spoke in Pennsylvania Dutch. He was one of the elders that held council with Bishop Bachman, and she knew he would carry news of this fire to the rest of the Amish Community. "If we hadn't seen the smoke when we did, the result would have been worse, ain't so?"

"*Ja,*" Ezekiel agreed. His intense gaze shifted from her to David and back again, obviously realizing the *Englischer* has been staying with her. "Have you had other trouble?"

She hesitated, then slowly nodded. "Several incidents have occurred in the past few days. I was hoping to discuss them with the bishop on Sunday, but he was busy."

"We will discuss this fire and the other incidents you've mentioned to understand what action must be taken," Ezekiel said firmly.

She quickly filled him in on the assault, the window watching and the cellar incident. The elder man's gaze grew more and more concerned. "You believe this is the work of one of our own?"

"I honestly don't know." Elizabeth wanted

to say yes, but really didn't have any basis to assert her opinion as fact.

"We will discuss this further among ourselves." Ezekiel Moore said. "Rest now, you appear exhausted."

"I am. *Denke*, your help and the others' were invaluable."

Ezekiel turned away. David followed him outside, but she couldn't move. It was as if she'd used every ounce of her strength to carry buckets, and didn't have anything left.

All too soon, she was forced to move when *Mammi* Ruth called down to find out what was going on.

"The fire is out," Elizabeth assured her. "We're safe. There's no threat to the house."

"But how did it start?" *Mammi* Ruth searched her gaze.

"I don't know. Ezekiel Moore was here and will be discussing this with Bishop Bachman." She knew mentioning the elders would put her mother-in-law at ease. "How are you feeling?"

"Fine." *Mammi* Ruth shifted in the bed. "I'd like to get up for a bit."

Elizabeth helped her out of bed, then heard her name being called from downstairs. The voice was female, and she smiled, knowing Leah Moore had come to check on her.

After helping *Mammi* Ruth come down the stairs and getting her settled in a chair near the woodburning stove, Elizabeth joined Leah in the kitchen.

"I brought dinner, for you." Leah put a hand on her arm. "That was a close call, ain't so?"

"Ja," Elizabeth agreed. "Certain sure God was looking out for us. Your *grosspappi* will discuss this with the bishop and other elders."

"I know, and that is very reassuring. Still, who could have done such a thing?" Leah's gaze was full of concern. "It seems danger is everywhere."

"But so is God," Elizabeth reminded her. She gave Leah a quick hug. "It's not up to us to figure out who is responsible. Certain sure the elders will take care of this issue."

Leah nodded and idly rubbed the area on her lower abdomen where she'd been stabbed two months ago. The assailant had mistaken Leah for Shauna, partially because Elizabeth had agreed to loan Shauna some Amish clothing to wear to hide from those trying to kill her. Elizabeth still carried guilt in the role she'd inadvertently played in Leah's being hurt. Although Leah had insisted neither Elizabeth nor Shauna were to blame.

"Is it true that David's home was recently destroyed by a fire as well?" Leah asked.

"Yes." Elizabeth shrugged. "It could be the same person is responsible for both fires."

"I believe Sheriff Harland should know about this fire, too," Leah confided. "I know it's not our way to involve outsiders, but your cousin did a wonderful job of saving Shauna and David back in October, *ja*?"

Elizabeth couldn't disagree. "Very much. Mayhap he'll learn something that will help the elders."

"That would be *sehr gut*." Leah gave her another hug, then moved toward the door. "Take care of yourself, Elizabeth."

"You, too." Elizabeth was about to close the door behind Leah, when she saw a familiar, dark SUV pull up. She grabbed her cloak and headed outside when she saw Liam slide out from behind the wheel. "*Ach*, cousin, how did you hear the news?"

"Um," Liam said, glancing at David, then back at her. Realization dawned. David had brought the cell phone back from the Amish Shoppe earlier that day. He must have called Liam to report the fire.

She squelched a flash of disappointment. It was true that this fire was likely started by the same man who'd destroyed David's home. But she would have preferred David to talk to her about involving her cousin in the investigation.

"I called him," David admitted. "I thought he should know about the similarities between the two fires."

She tried not to sigh too loudly as she turned toward her cousin. "Ezekiel Moore is planning to discuss this event and the other incidents with the elders."

"Is he still here?" Liam asked. "I'd like to talk to him and the others who worked hard to douse the fire."

"They won't talk to you, Liam." She couldn't help being exasperated. This was exactly why it was pointless for David to have called him.

"I know, but I have to try." Liam arched a brow. "You want the person responsible caught, don't you? What if the fire had spread to the house? You and your mother-in-law would have no place to live."

"Yes." Of course she wanted the perpetrator caught, but if he was Amish, like she secretly believed he was, the punishment would come from within the community. Not from *Englisch* law enforcement.

"It can't hurt for him to ask for information,"

David said. "As Liam said, we are blessed that the fire didn't reach the house."

She threw up her hands. "*Ach*, do what you will. But know it will be a waste of time."

As she turned to head back inside, Liam called, "Elizabeth? My offer for you, Ruth and David to stay with me and Shauna is still open. The danger is very real, and I want you to be safe."

And just like that, her anger and frustration drained away. Even though Liam's parents had left the Amish community years ago, he still tried to look out for her. "*Denke*, Liam. But I think we'll be fine, *ja*? The person who did this chose the empty barn to burn, rather than the house."

"Yeah, something I find curious," Liam admitted. "If this is the work of Bryon Wells, why set the barn on fire in the afternoon and use the barn as the focal point? If the goal was to take lives, waiting until nighttime and setting fire to the house would have been a better choice."

His observation made her shiver. "You raise interesting questions, Liam. Unfortunately, I don't have any answers for you."

"I also think it's strange that the southwest corner of the barn was used as the source of the fire," David said. "The wind was coming from the east, which worked in our favor in fighting the blaze. If he'd chosen an eastern-facing corner, the fire may have spread more quickly beneath the force of the wind."

"But the southwest corner is hidden from view of the house," Liam pointed out. "It may have been more important for the arsonist to stay out of sight."

"Maybe," David agreed.

She sighed. "Go, ask your questions then. I hope you find some answers. You're welcome to stay for dinner, Leah Moore has supplied us with the evening meal."

"Shauna's waiting for me, but thanks for the offer." Liam turned toward David. "Let's see if we can get anyone to talk."

Elizabeth left them to it, heading back inside. She closed the door and leaned against it for a long moment, before removing her cloak.

"What's going on?" *Mammi* Ruth asked.

"Nothing for you to worry about." Elizabeth forced a smile. "Leah Moore brought dinner. Are you hungry? I can heat up the soup anytime."

"Sehr gut," the older woman agreed.

As Elizabeth made the preparations for the evening meal, she could see David and Liam attempting to talk to the Amish men who'd helped fight the blaze.

Both men were outsiders to the community. It was disappointing that David's alliance with Liam would set him back in the progress he'd made with the elders.

A stark reminder that when the danger was over, she'd move on with her life, without David McKay at her side.

David hated knowing how he'd once again upset Elizabeth. But he'd done what he thought was right. A plan that had pretty much backfired. He was *Englisch* enough to call the police when facing a legal concern.

A habit that he was finding difficult to break.

The Amish elders shook their heads and turned away one by one, without providing any insight into who may have started the fire. Even Jacob Strauss had turned away without saying a word, closing the door of his house behind him. David feared he'd never be welcomed into the community if he continued pressing the issue.

"Elizabeth was right, that was futile," Liam muttered. "We've got nothing to go on."

He stared over at the partially collapsed

barn. "It's different than the fire set at my place. The location where the fire started was different, along with the lack of an accelerant being used."

"I'm no arson investigation expert, but let's take a closer look at the point of origin." Liam headed toward the southwest corner of the barn. He knelt on the ground and sniffed around the area. "You're right. I don't smell any kerosene, gas or lighter fluid."

"The fire was small when I got here, but the wood was dry and burning pretty fast." David scrubbed his hands over his face. "I never felt so helpless. Fighting the fire with buckets of water—" He shook his head, the aftermath of the close call hitting hard. It was impressive how the Amish had come together in a time of crisis. Even Jacob, a man who still resided on the top of his suspect list as being responsible for some of the incidents. "I can't believe we managed to get the fire under control."

"You did good, David." Liam clapped him on the back. "I just wish Elizabeth would reconsider coming to stay with me."

"It's because of *Mammi* Ruth." He grimaced. "She's pretty set in her ways, doesn't think much of me. Or maybe she just doesn't like any outsider."

"I guess I can understand her desire to cling to the old ways," Liam said diplomatically. "But I really don't like this. Whoever this guy is, he's escalating."

David didn't much like it, either. "If we stick with the theory of an Amish perpetrator and an *Englisch* one, then it seems logical to believe someone within the Amish community started this fire. Jacob came over to help put the fire out, but it wouldn't be the first time that the suspect pretended to play the hero by rushing to the rescue."

"But again, what's his motive?" Liam asked.

"That one I haven't figured out. But what is interesting is that the rusty plow that was used to trap us in the cellar was put back in its rightful place while we were at the Amish Shoppe this morning." He gestured for Liam to follow him to the yard. "That's it, over there."

"That does lead me to think he's involved," Liam admitted. "But he's also not going to talk to either of us. You'll have to convince Elizabeth to share her suspicions about Jacob to the Amish elders, if she hasn't done so already. Maybe they can find out something we've missed."

"Yeah, I'll do that."

"Look, I have to go," Liam said. "But I want

you to know that I'm going to ask deputies to drive past Elizabeth's place on a regular basis."

"The Amish will see them and possibly look down upon Elizabeth," David said with a frown.

"Yeah, but I'll ask them to use their personal vehicles. That may not draw as much attention."

David walked Liam back to the SUV. "Thanks, Liam."

"You're welcome. Keep the women safe, okay?"

"I will." Once Liam drove away, he headed back inside. He noticed the pot of soup Elizabeth had left on the stove, but there was no sign of either woman. It wasn't that late, but he didn't doubt Elizabeth was still upset with him for calling Liam.

He cleaned the soot from his hands and face, then headed over to help himself to a bowl of soup and a thick slice of bread. He was famished, but sat alone at the table, his head bowed. He silently prayed for God's blessing, especially in keeping Elizabeth and *Mammi* Ruth safe from harm.

He might deserve the revenge Bryon Wells sought to level upon his head, but Elizabeth and *Mammi* Ruth did not.

"*Ach*, I didn't hear you come in." Elizabeth came over to join him at the table. "Leah's soup tastes *sehr gut, ja?*"

"I haven't tried it yet." He was relieved she was speaking to him. "I'm sure it's great, but not as good as yours."

"I'm not the cook Leah, is," she chided. "If I had to run the Sunshine Café, I'd be forced to close down in less than a week, ain't so?"

"Doubtful." He would always defend her, although he had to admit Leah's soup hit the spot. He tried to gauge Elizabeth's mood. "Is *Mammi* Ruth okay?"

"*Ja.*" She frowned. "I meant to seek the doctor's counsel, but the fire distracted me. Two falls in as many days makes me think something more is going on with her."

"I hope it's nothing serious." He continued eating, content to have a bit of alone time with Elizabeth.

"*Ach*, me, too." She slowly rose to her feet. "It's been a long day. I hope you don't mind if I retire early."

"Of course not." He could tell her muscles were stiff and sore by the way she moved. He'd been impressed with her ability to continuously pump water for him to use on the fire. "Good night, Elizabeth."

"Good night." She turned and headed back upstairs.

He finished eating, then took a few minutes to wash the dishes. It wasn't until he was stretched out on the sofa beneath Elizabeth's quilt that he remembered he hadn't finished examining the interior of the closet. The space looked empty, but he'd rather verify that by inspecting it more closely.

While he was still curious, he was also physically spent. Besides, if he headed up there now, he'd likely wake Elizabeth and *Mammi* Ruth.

He told himself waiting until morning wouldn't hurt. And maybe the timing would be better, then. If there was anything significant hidden inside, they could take it straight to Bishop Bachman.

David closed his eyes and relaxed. Knowing that Liam had deputies driving by to keep an eye on the place reassured him. He'd considered staying awake himself, but fighting the fire had worn him out.

Thirty-six wasn't that old, but he was feeling every year today.

He had barely fallen asleep when a creaking sound woke him. Remembering the fire and the cellar, he sat bolt upright, his heart pounding. He didn't hesitate to pull out the mobile phone to call Liam. It didn't matter if Elizabeth was angry with him, as long as she was safe.

"David?" Liam sounded sleepy. "What's going on?"

"I think someone is outside." He stood and moved toward the door. He heard another sound from outside. "Send someone, quickly," he whispered, then tucked the phone away.

The front door swung open and an Amish man strode in. It only took David a second to recognize Luke Embers, but what kept him frozen in place was the gun in his hand.

"Be quiet, or I'll shoot," Luke said.

Luke, not Jacob. Stunned, David raised his hands, in a gesture of goodwill. "What do you want? You can take whatever you need. There's no reason to shoot anyone."

"I want what Adam owes me," Luke said in a low, fierce tone. "The money and the drugs."

Drugs? David gaped at him. "Why would Adam have money and drugs?"

Luke let out a harsh laugh. "Because we were in business together. A very lucrative one at that, thanks to the *Englischers* who desire drugs. Only he was getting cold feet and wanted to quit." Luke sneered. "Now hand it over!"

David didn't so much as glance at the stairway heading up to the second floor. No doubt if there really were drugs and money left behind, it was cleverly hidden in the apparently empty closet.

Yet David didn't believe Luke would simply take the stash and walk away. No, he had to realize that Elizabeth would go straight to Bishop Bachman and the elders. Desperation had brought Luke here; he wouldn't leave without a fight.

He drew in a deep breath and let it out slowly. He would stop Luke from getting anywhere near the women.

Even if that meant sacrificing himself.

FIFTEEN

Near the top of the stairs, Elizabeth gasped in horror. Money? Drugs? Luke and Adam were in business together?

Illegal business?

Deep down, she realized she should have known. *Ach*, she'd sensed something was amiss. Her marriage to Adam had not been what she'd expected, but she'd never gone as far as believing Adam was a criminal.

But he clearly had been.

"Are you the one who hit me over the head in the barn?" David asked.

"I wanted you gone." Luke's emotionless statement sent chills down her spine. "But you wouldn't leave, and Elizabeth refused to court me, so here we are."

"You were searching the barn, then the cellar for the drugs and money, right?"

"You're so smart," Luke jeered.

"Why did you start the fire in the barn?" David asked.

"I was thinking you and Elizabeth might leave the house, but my plan didn't work. And I'm tired of waiting. I'm here to take what is rightfully mine. The sooner you hand it over, the better."

"I'm happy to help you take what is yours. I can guarantee Elizabeth wants nothing to do with drugs or drug money. But Luke, you need to put the gun down," David said.

She appreciated David's calm, rational tone, and his attempt to reason with Luke. If that was even possible. Even from up here, she could tell Luke was on edge. Was it possible Luke used some of the drugs himself? Was that why he was acting so strangely? Adam's cousin had a gun, while all David had was a knife.

And she felt certain David would do everything possible to avoid hurting Luke. Especially after the way he'd accidently killed Carson Wells six years ago. She wasn't sure David could handle knowing he'd killed another man, even in self-defense.

A flash of anger hit hard. All of this hurt and terror over ill-gotten gains? Searching her barn, the cellar, her house, just to find what Adam had hidden from him?

"You killed Adam, didn't you?" David said.

She clamped a hand over her mouth to muffle her gasp.

"That was truly an accident," Luke said. "We fought and I pushed him a little too hard." Luke paused, then said, "*Ach*, now I realize you know too much, *Englischer*."

The dire threat was impossible to ignore. Time was running out. She needed to do something, anything to convince Luke to leave them alone.

Elizabeth silently eased back from the top of the stairs, her heart pounding. She quickly went into the spare room toward the closet she and David had broken open earlier that day. It was dark, and she hadn't brought a lantern. Thankfully, there was some moonlight filtering through the windows.

Yet, as she pushed the door aside and entered the empty closet, she found it was much darker inside. She took a moment to let her eyes adjust, but it didn't help. She'd gotten a brief glimpse earlier, before *Mammi* Ruth fell, and before the barn fire. The space had seemed empty, with just one wall of bare shelves.

Remembering how Adam had talked about putting in a trap door from the cellar to the kitchen, she wondered if he'd done that here.

She knelt on the floor, and felt along the wooden planks.

The wood was smooth, but then she found a small indentation. Tucking her fingertips into the groove, she pulled.

A small section of the closet floor lifted.

Her throat tightened as she felt inside the small opening that had been revealed. She found two items, a tightly bound wad of money and a small cardboard box likely containing the drugs Luke mentioned.

It made her sick to realize this had been hidden in here this entire time. That Adam had purposefully brought drugs and drug money into their home.

But there wasn't time to worry about that now. She had what Luke had come for.

Time to make a trade.

Even as the thought entered her mind, she knew it wouldn't be easy. Luke had admitted his intent to kill them all, which seemed inconceivable. No one would believe their deaths to be anything but murder, especially after the fire.

Then again, he could possibly stage the entire thing to place the blame on David. She'd heard of murder suicides that happened in the *Englisch* world. David was an outsider and would readily be viewed as a suspect by the Amish community.

No. She had to find a way to prevent that from happening.

Could she convince Luke to leave the Amish community, disappear from the Green Lake area to live somewhere else? Maybe.

It was the only plan she could come up with.

She lifted the box and the wad of money from the hiding space. She quickly opened the box, which wasn't sealed, and stuffed the money inside. She didn't look any further, not wanting to know what sorts of drugs were inside.

With only one item to carry, she headed back to the top of the stairs. There had to be a way to convince Luke to take the items and leave, without harming them.

Dear Lord, please keep us safe in Your care!

Taking a deep breath, she slowly took one step down, then another, hugging the wall to stay hidden. She thought about throwing them at Luke as a diversion, but her arms were still so weary and sore from hauling water to fight the fire that she feared the items would drop uselessly to the floor and nowhere near Luke.

She added another prayer that God might grant her the strength she'd need to accomplish the task before her. In that moment, she felt a sense of peace. Death wasn't something to fear; she would have everlasting life with her Lord.

Yet she also felt a keen regret that she wouldn't have the chance to explore a possible future with David.

After taking two more steps down, she could see David standing a few feet from Luke, standing a bit to the side, giving her a good view of the ugly and lethal pistol Luke was pointing at David's chest.

Handguns weren't common among the Amish. Rifles for hunting, yes, but not handguns. She tested the weight of the box, wondering if there was a weapon inside, along with the drugs. It didn't seem that heavy.

At this point, she wouldn't put anything past her deceased husband.

"Move, now!" Luke said curtly.

"Okay, okay." David stood with his hands lifted chest high, his palms out. Even from here, she could tell David had no intention of letting Luke head upstairs. Her chest tightened with panic as she understood David would sacrifice himself to save her.

She took one more step down, then paused, gauging the distance between where she stood and Luke.

It was farther away than she would have

liked. The cardboard box was too big for her to throw with one hand, so she eased down one more step and lifted the box over her head with both hands. Her arm muscles quivered and screamed in pain, but she ignored it and threw the box toward Luke with all the strength she could muster.

The box sailed toward Luke at the same moment a loud crash reverberated through the room. She thought there might be a gun inside the box that had accidently gone off, but then saw Jacob standing inside the front door, his facial features etched with anger.

Her heart plummeted to the bottom of her feet. Of course, she should have realized Jacob was in on it, too. Why else would he and Luke have argued over courting her?

It all made a sick sort of sense.

Luke glanced toward the box on the floor, then moved the gun just a bit as he looked toward Jacob. Taking advantage of that momentary hesitation, David lunged toward Luke.

"No! David!" She nearly fell down the last few stairs to reach him.

A crack of gunfire reverberating through the room had her ducking for cover, even as she prayed.

Please, Lord, spare David's life!

* * *

David heard the gunfire, fully expecting to be hit with a bullet. Yet there was no pain as his body slammed into Luke.

He'd seen Jacob burst in through the front door and knew he was outnumbered. Yet that didn't stop him.

The box that had come sailing past must have been from Elizabeth. Which meant he was the only person between these two men and her.

Luke's head made a sickening thud as he hit the floor. David wrestled the gun from Luke's hand and quickly rolled off the fallen Amish man to face Jacob. In the back of his mind, he battled a wave of nausea at the thought he might have knocked Luke's head to the ground with enough force to kill him.

The same way he'd killed Carson Wells.

"Don't move!" The shout was more of a croak. "I don't want to hurt you!"

To his surprise, Jacob nodded, sweeping his gaze over the area. Then he slowly lifted his arms up over his head. "I'm not armed."

David wasn't sure if he should believe him. He glanced at Luke, the knot in his stomach intensifying as he realized the guy wasn't moving.

No, please, Lord, no. Not again! Please, not again!

"Jacob, take the money and the drugs," Elizabeth pleaded. "Then go, just leave us alone."

Jacob didn't move for a long moment, then turned back to look at him. "I came to stop Luke, but I see you have it under control."

"To stop Luke?" He stared at the Amish man. "How did you know?"

Jacob grimaced. "I didn't know, but I had concerns. Suspicions. Luke and Adam had grown close, but they also argued on a regular basis. Adam was my friend, but he'd grown secretive over the year before his death. I had a bad feeling Adam had gone down a dark path."

"You suspected he was a criminal?" Elizabeth wrapped her arms around her torso as if chilled. Jacob must have noticed, because he stepped inside and closed the door behind him. "*Ach*, why didn't you tell me?"

"I didn't have proof." Jacob's gaze swung toward the cardboard box that had split open upon landing. A tightly wadded bundle of money and several bags of white powder could be seen inside. "Now I do."

"So why seek to court Elizabeth?" David asked. He wanted to believe Jacob wasn't involved, but he wasn't ready to trust him yet. "All you did was frighten her more."

Jacob's scowl deepened. "My intent was to protect her as I feared she might be in danger. I always suspected Adam's death wasn't an accident."

"It wasn't," David said. "Luke admitted to hitting him too hard."

"*Denke* for your concern, Jacob, but certain sure it would have been more help to tell me of your doubts," Elizabeth said. "All this time, I feared you were the person who pushed me to the ground and trapped us in the cellar beneath your rusty plow."

"Trapped in the cellar?" The shock on Jacob's face looked genuine. "Was that why the plow was lying along the side of your house?"

"Yes, the door slammed down on us, and Luke used the plow to prevent us from getting out," David said.

"David used all his strength to free us," Elizabeth added. "If he wasn't successful, we would have suffered hypothermia and probable death."

"I didn't know." Jacob's low voice was full of regret.

David sighed and lowered the gun. But then

quickly jerked it up as the front door opened again. "Liam?"

"David, are you and Elizabeth okay?" Liam held his gun ready as he swept his gaze over the room. He quickly holstered the gun and grabbed Jacob's wrists, yanking them behind his back. "Jacob Strauss, you're under arrest for arson, assault and attempted murder," Liam said.

"No, Liam, it's not Jacob," Elizabeth hurried over to stop her cousin from arresting her neighbor. "Please, the person who did these things is Luke Embers, not Jacob."

"She's right, Luke pretty much confessed." David dropped to his knees to check Luke's pulse. For a long horrible moment he didn't feel anything. An icy wave of dread hit hard, but then the rapid beat of Luke's heartbeat fluttered beneath his fingertips.

He bowed his head and whispered, "Thank You, Lord."

"David?" Elizabeth hurried to his side. When she realized Luke was still alive, she wrapped her arm around his shoulders. *"Denke,"* she said in a low voice. "Certain sure, you saved my life."

He shook his head. "Your decision to throw the box toward Luke as a distraction is what saved us both." He covered her hand with his. "That and Jacob's timely arrival."

"Certain sure, I never expected Luke," she agreed. As if hearing her voice, the man on the floor stirred.

"Let's get back." David slowly rose and drew her away from the fallen Amish man. He didn't trust him not to come upright, swinging his fists. Thankfully, the gun was well out of reach.

But Luke only groaned and lifted a hand to his head.

"You're not hurt?" Elizabeth asked, searching David's gaze. "When the gun went off…" She didn't finish.

"I'm fine." He glanced down to his torso to be sure. He knew from his stint in jail that adrenaline had a way of masking pain. It was only after the adrenaline rush passed that you felt every blow that had been landed.

"I'll take Luke into custody," Liam said, coming over to join them. "If you're sure he confessed."

"I heard him," Elizabeth said. "He was determined to get the money and drugs he claimed Adam had stolen from him."

Liam hiked a brow. "That money and drugs, I presume?" He gestured toward the partially open box on the floor.

"Yes, I found it in a secret compartment in the closet floor." She managed a weary smile. "I believe God was guiding me, because it was too dark to see, but I found the ridge with my fingertips and managed to open the compartment."

"Well, that certainly explains a few things," Liam said. "I have reason to believe Luke was the Amish man who was seen inside the Green Lake Grill. Garrett recently discovered there are several drug deals going on there. Seems to be a hub of illegal activity."

David thought about the man in the ski mask who'd shot at him after he left the restaurant. "Do you think Luke is the shooter, then?"

"I don't know the answer to that yet. The investigation is still ongoing." Liam clasped one handcuff around Luke's wrist as the man blinked and opened his eyes, looking around in confusion. Liam grinned with satisfaction. "We have Bryon Wells in custody."

"You do?" David was stunned, but he wasn't the only one shocked to hear the news.

"What?" Luke looked dazed. "Bryon? You arrested Bryon?"

David scowled at the man who'd nearly killed him. The link between the Amish and *Englisch* was suddenly very clear. "Well, now, isn't this interesting. And how is it exactly that you're on a first-name basis with Bryon Wells?"

Luke flushed, reaching up to rub the back of his head. "*Ach*, I'm not. I've only heard about him, that's all."

"Yeah, right. I'm not buying that for a hot second, as Bryon is singing like a canary to get himself a lighter sentence. But that's okay, I'd rather you don't say anything more," Liam warned. "Luke Embers, you're under arrest. You have the right to remain silent. Anything you say can and will be used against you in a court of law."

"*Englisch* law," Luke sneered, scoffing at Liam's reciting of the Miranda warning. "I'm not going anywhere with you. My actions will only be judged by the Amish leaders, not you outsiders."

"Wrong answer," Liam said cheerfully. "You are under arrest and I am taking you into custody." Liam hauled Luke to his feet and cuffed his wrists behind his back. "Thanks to the chat I've had with Bryon Wells, I have every reason to believe you've been involved in dealing drugs outside the Amish community, not to mention being hired by Bryon to come after David and Elizabeth. Something that worked to your advantage, since it provided money and opportunity to find the missing money and drugs. Both of those actions grant me the right to hold you accountable to our laws. So again, I advise you to keep your mouth shut."

"Stop him," Luke said, glaring at Jacob. "This isn't how things are done among the Amish, Jacob."

"No, I won't stop him. Because he's right," Jacob said grimly. "Do you honestly believe the Amish elders will want anything to do with you when they hear about how you've been dealing drugs? And being hired to extract revenge? That's not just burning down a neighbor's barn, or assaulting one of our own, which is bad enough. Those charges are very serious and fall well outside the purview of the Amish community. Something you should have considered before you decided to deal drugs to make easy money, rather than doing honest work to make a living." Jacob waved a dismissive hand. "Go and don't look back. You will be banished and shunned from the community when the elders hear the news."

"But…" Luke protested weakly.

"Silence," Liam commanded. "I don't want to hear another word, understand?"

Luke finally clamped his mouth shut as Liam pulled him toward the door. Liam turned to glance over his shoulder. "Oh, and David? Don't let anyone touch the drugs or the money. I'll return in a few minutes to get the evidence once I have him secured in my vehicle."

"That's not a problem." David let out a long breath and turned toward the tall Amish man. "Jacob, I owe you an apology."

"No, you don't." Jacob eyed him steadily. "I saw the way you threw yourself at Luke. I admire your courage, *Englischer*. And I applaud your intent to protect Elizabeth from harm." There was a flash of regret that darkened Jacob's eyes. Was it possible the stern-faced Amish man regretted scaring Elizabeth? Or maybe he truly had romantic feelings for her.

Not that he could blame him. After all, David had fallen in love with her, too.

Love. He loved her. *He loved her!* More than he'd ever thought possible.

But now their time together would come to an end. She would be safe now that the money and drugs had been taken away, and Luke had been arrested.

In fact, he believed Jacob would continue to watch out for Elizabeth after he was gone.

"I need to go," Jacob said. He turned, then

hesitated. "*Denke*, David, for everything you've done."

David managed a weary smile. "Thanks to you, too, Jacob. Your arrival helped distract Luke when we needed it the most."

Jacob gave a slight nod, then left. A moment later, Liam returned to place the drugs and money into an evidence bag. "I'll be in touch tomorrow. We may have more information to share on the so-called arrangement between Bryon Wells and Luke Embers, by then."

"Sounds good." David shut the door behind Liam and finally turned toward Elizabeth. "I'm glad the danger is finally over."

"Certain sure," she agreed, moving toward him. She wrapped her arms around his waist and hugged him. "I'm so relieved you weren't hurt."

"I feel the same about you." He wanted nothing more than to gather her close, but forced himself to keep their embrace brief. "Now, try to get some sleep."

"That will be impossible." She searched his gaze. "What is it, David?"

Before he could think of a way to respond, he heard *Mammi* Ruth calling from upstairs. "You need to check on your mother-in-law," he said. "I'm sure she heard the commotion down here."

Elizabeth didn't so much as glance toward the stairs. "There is much we need to discuss, *ja?*"

"Yes, but it can wait until the morning." He moved back, encouraging her to head upstairs.

Elizabeth finally turned away, and David waited for her to get up to the second floor before sinking down on the edge of the sofa.

Holding back from hugging and kissing Elizabeth was the hardest thing he'd ever done. But he knew it was for the best.

Elizabeth's future was here with the Amish, and despite how keenly he wished otherwise, he would never be anything but an outsider. He sat with his head in his hands for long minutes, wishing things were different. Then he stood, removed the phone from his pocket and prepared to stretch out on the sofa.

He heard something from outside, and swallowed a groan. No doubt Liam or one of the deputies had come back with more questions. He crossed to the front door and opened it. A quick sweeping glance revealed a large black truck parked off to the side of the road.

The image of the black truck he'd seen leaving the Amish Shoppe flashed in his mind. Before he could react, an older man stepped out from the shadows. And for the second time that night, David found himself at the wrong end of a gun.

He froze as the man stepped closer. "Who are you? What do you want?"

The instant he asked, he knew. There was enough of a family resemblance in the facial features between this man and Carson Wells.

This had to be Marvin Wells, Carson's father.

SIXTEEN

After providing *Mammi* Ruth with an abbreviated version of what had transpired downstairs, one that did not put Adam in a bad light, she decided to head back downstairs to talk to David.

She didn't want to wait until morning. She wouldn't be able to sleep anytime soon, and doubted he would, either. So why not talk now?

Watching David sacrifice himself for her when he'd lunged at Luke had been humbling. She knew in that moment that she loved him.

Loved David in the way she hadn't been able to love Adam.

David's warm embrace, his reverent kiss made her realize how much had been missing from her marriage. Never before had she wanted to kiss a man the way she did David.

Yet she sensed she was losing him. David would think his leaving was honorable, that he was the outsider unable to ever be fully accepted by the Amish community. It was his past that haunted him, making him feel unworthy.

She fully intended to prove him wrong. Especially in light of everything that had transpired with Luke Embers, a man who had been Amish. An upbringing that hadn't prevented him from turning to a life of crime.

The same thing Adam had done, too.

Yet David was the one with a criminal past, she silently acknowledged. What did it matter? She held David in higher esteem than she did Luke or Adam.

David had fully repented his sins. A man who followed God's path was one worth fighting for. David's future was in the hands of Bishop Bachman and the elders, yet she would do her part to let them know how David had protected her from harm. Surely his good deeds and the way he'd embraced the Amish lifestyle would be enough for Bishop Bachman to grant his blessing in welcoming David to the community.

Even if David didn't reciprocate her feelings, she wanted him to feel as if he belonged.

She went down the stairs, but stopped at the halfway point when she realized David was standing in the open doorway. A chill that had nothing to do with the cold December temperatures shimmered down her spine.

Something was wrong.

"There's no need to come any closer," David said. His calm voice did nothing to ease her concern. "You're the man with the gun. I'll come with you peacefully."

"Fine. Take two steps forward." The gravelly voice was one she'd never heard before. "And don't try anything foolish, or I'll kill you right here."

No! Please, God, not again! Save David!

Moments after David closed the front door behind him, she rushed down the stairs. She was about to yank the door open, then hesitated. The man had a gun and she did not have a single doubt that he'd use it.

What could she do? The back door! She could run through the backyard to find Jacob. Did she have enough time? She didn't know, but had to try.

What other option was there?

As she whirled around, her gaze landed on the cell phone David had left behind. Yes! Without hesitation, she scooped it up and dialed 911.

"What's the nature of your emergency?" a calm voice asked.

"There's a gunman holding David McKay at gunpoint outside my house." She rattled off her address. "Please, hurry! He's threatening to kill David! Let Sheriff Harland know!"

"Please stay on the line," the voice replied.

Elizabeth carried the phone across the room and peered through the window. The two men were walking toward a large black truck.

"He's driving a black pickup truck! Hurry!"

"I've placed the call. Deputies will be responding shortly."

Elizabeth wanted to scream in frustration. Deep down, she knew they would be too late.

She debated whether or not to run and fetch Jacob for assistance, but knew his horse and buggy wouldn't be able to catch up with a powerful truck. The deputies would have a better chance.

Feeling helpless, she raised her eyes up to the ceiling and prayed with all her heart that David would be all right.

"Where are you taking me?" David asked. He walked slowly, desperate to find a way to escape. He still had Liam's knife, but digging it out of his pocket would be too noticeable. The only good news was that Elizabeth and Ruth were safely tucked away upstairs.

It bothered him, though, that he wouldn't have the opportunity to tell Elizabeth how much he loved her. He never should have sent her upstairs, promising to talk in the morning.

Based on Marvin's holding him at gunpoint, he likely wouldn't have tomorrow.

"What does it matter?" Marvin gestured toward the truck with his gun. "You're not going to live long enough to care."

"You intend to kill me."

"I have to," Marvin said in a cold one. "You killed my boy."

"I know. And I'm sorry. Killing Carson was not my intent. I only wanted him to stop grabbing a young woman who wasn't interested."

"Yeah, I know the story you blabbed to the police back then." Marvin's voice was full of disbelief. "I don't care what your *intent* was. My son is dead, by your hand. It's only fair for you to die, too. You see that, don't you?"

Maybe the guy was grieving his son, but his logic was truly warped. "No, I don't see that. But I'm not afraid to die, for those who believe in Jesus Christ will be granted eternal life. You're the one who will have to learn to live with blood staining your hands. The way I had to."

"Don't give me that God stuff," Marvin sneered. "Dead is dead." He let out a humorless laugh. "As you'll soon find out for yourself."

"Bryon has been arrested," David said bluntly. "Killing me will be for nothing. You've lost two sons now."

"Nah, I'll get Bryon out. My slick lawyers will take this hick-town sheriff apart in no time. Now move!"

"You don't want my blood on your hands," he tried again.

"Oh, I think I'll sleep just fine."

A flash of pity for the man washed over him. Marvin's determination to seek revenge would likely haunt him for years to come.

"Hurry up and get inside." Marvin had stopped near the truck and waved his gun impatiently. "We need to get out of here."

David hesitated, instinctively knowing that climbing inside would seal his death warrant. He'd been honest in saying he wasn't afraid to die, yet he yearned for one last conversation with Elizabeth. If only he hadn't sent her away without telling her how he felt. How much he loved her.

But then, she'd have been in danger, too.

It was better this way. He hoped Elizabeth would find the happiness she deserved.

"David!"

For a nanosecond he thought he imagined her voice, but when Marvin's gaze darted past his shoulder, he knew it was real. Marvin turned his gun toward the sound.

"No!" A red haze of fury filled his vision, much like the one he'd experienced that night he'd punched Carson. He threw himself at Marvin, batting at the gun just as gunfire echoed around them.

The older man was no match for David's anger-fueled strength. He crashed to the ground with a low groan beneath David's weight. David wrenched the gun from Marvin's hand and tossed it aside. Then he lifted his fist to punch him. To make him pay…

The red haze of anger abruptly faded, and he found himself staring into Marvin's frightened face.

He slowly lowered his fist, letting out a low breath. Then he pressed harder down on the guy, with all his weight. "You're not going to kill anyone, understand?"

"David! Are you okay?" Another voice— a man's, not Elizabeth's—reached him. He kept Marvin pinned to the ground as Garrett Nichol, Liam's chief deputy, rushed forward. "You can move off him now, I'll take it from here." Garrett took a set of handcuffs off his belt and used them to bind Marvin Wells's wrists.

"How did you know Marvin was here?" David slowly rose to his feet. He thought he felt the impact of a bullet, so he ran his hands over his torso.

"Elizabeth called it in." Garrett grinned. "That's the second time in the past two months that she's saved your hide."

David managed a smile. Garrett was right, Elizabeth had sounded the alarm after he'd been kidnapped. And again, now.

"David? Are you hurt?" Elizabeth rushed forward, her gaze raking over him.

"I—don't think so." He wasn't sure how he'd managed to avoid being shot twice in one night. Had to be that God was truly watching over him. "You called Garrett?"

"*Ach*, of course I did! I saw you walking away with the *Englisch* gunman." She looked annoyed that he was questioning him. Then her eyes welled with tears and she threw herself into his arms. It took him a moment to realize she was sobbing.

"Shh, it's okay, Elizabeth. I'm fine. Everything is going to be all right." He crushed her close, the way he'd wanted to do earlier.

Only this time, he wasn't sure he'd find the strength to let her go.

"I knew you would sacrifice yourself for me again, ain't so?" She sniffled loudly and raised her head to look up at him. In the moonlight he could see the dampness on her cheeks. He reached up and used the pad of his thumb to wipe them away.

"Always," he admitted. "You're very important to me. Besides, I promised I would keep you safe."

"You're important to me, too. I'm so glad you're not hurt." Elizabeth managed a smile. "But this is enough excitement for the night, *ja*? There's no more danger, is there?"

"We have Bryon Wells in custody, and his daddy, Marvin, will soon join him," Garrett assured her. Then he glanced at David with a grimace. "I'm only sorry we didn't realize Marvin was here in Green Lake, as well. If we had, we would have tracked him down before now."

"It's okay." David noticed Marvin's gaze remained downcast, his shoulders slumped, as if he knew he'd failed in his mission to extract revenge for his son's death. "He intended to kill me, and my only goal was to keep him from hurting Elizabeth and *Mammi* Ruth."

"I figured as much," Garrett admitted.

"He claims to have slick lawyers that will be no match for you and Liam, but I don't believe that anyone can help them now," David said.

"We've got the evidence we need to put them both away for a long time," Garrett assured him.

"I'm glad it's over for real this time." He found it ironic that both father and son would go to jail, the way he had for killing their son. A strange circle of justice.

"Me, too." Garrett tugged at Marvin's bound arms. "Come with me, Wells. You're under arrest for the attempted murder of David McKay. You have the right to remain silent. Everything you say can and will be used against you in a court of law."

David tuned Garrett out, focusing only on Elizabeth. "Let's get you inside, it's freezing out here."

She nodded and reluctantly pulled out of his arms.

"I almost punched him in the face, the same way I hit his son six years ago," David said in a low voice. "That isn't something an Amish man would do."

"Almost, doesn't count, ain't so?" Elizabeth walked into the living room, then turned to face him. "I prayed you wouldn't lose your temper and you didn't."

He nodded slowly, remembering that brief second he'd nearly hit Wells. "I'm glad I managed to maintain control. And I truly hope that I'll be accepted into the Amish community, despite my past."

"*Ach*, David, you must know that you're a different man now than you were six years ago," she chided. "Certain sure you have the strength and courage God has given you. Think about it, you were held at gunpoint twice tonight and only acted to save others."

It was difficult to argue with her statement, although he didn't think his intentions were really that honorable. But it was true that he was a very different man than the one who'd struck Carson Wells with enough force to kill him. He liked to believe he was the man who'd chosen to follow God's path, one that had led him here to this moment with Elizabeth.

"I want to become fully Amish, Elizabeth. This is something I've wanted for a long time, since opening my woodworking shop." He hesitated, then asked, "Be honest. Do you think Bishop Bachman will approve?"

"*Ja*, I believe so. You have been attending

our services for well over a year, ain't so? But for now, will you please kiss me again?"

He blinked in surprise, but before his brain could come up with a coherent response, she stepped into his arms and kissed him.

He pulled her close and kissed her with all the emotion he'd kept bottled inside over these past few months. He loved her sweet taste, the softness of her lips, the way she fit so perfectly in his arms.

When they needed to breathe, he reluctantly lifted his head and tried to pull his scattered thoughts together. "I don't know what to say."

"I do." Elizabeth gazed up at him. "I love you, David. I tried not to, as I wasn't willing to give up my independence, but in truth, that was simply an excuse."

She loved him? His heart swelled with hope, but he forced himself to ask, "Are you sure? I'm still a criminal, and I killed a man. No matter how hard I try to pretend otherwise, I will always carry that guilt with me."

"*Ach*, David, God has forgiven your sins long ago." She pinned him with an intense gaze. "Don't you think it's time for you to forgive yourself?"

"I—uh, maybe." He thought about that for a moment. He knew God had forgiven him—the events that had unfolded tonight proved that. God had saved him more than once.

But forgiving himself wasn't nearly as easy.

"I love you, David," Elizabeth said again. "I hope you will continue to stay with us over the Christmas holiday."

He nodded and let go of the lingering doubts. "I love you, too, Elizabeth. I have been in love with you for a while, now. But I need you to be sure." He frowned. "It will not be an easy path. We will need to talk to the bishop about my ability to become Amish, and our court-ship and ultimately our marriage."

"Marriage?" Was it his imagination or was there a hint of panic in her brown eyes. Then she smiled. "*Ach*, is that your way of asking me to marry you?"

"I—uh…" He flushed. "Sorry, I know I cannot ask for your hand until the bishop grants permission for me to become Amish."

"*Ja*, that is true," she admitted. "When will you talk to him?"

"As soon as possible." He couldn't help but smile. "I was going to ask him this past Sunday, but my fears over being rejected by my past held me back."

"Ach, David, give Bishop Bachman some

credit to know the man you are today, not who you once were."

He wanted to believe she was right. "I hope so." He kissed her again, then lifted her head. "I have emulated the Amish lifestyle for a long time, I will continue to pray Bishop Bachman will allow me to become baptized."

She seemed to consider that for a moment. "My wish for you, David, is for you to have a place to belong. And certain sure, that place is here within our community. I love you so much, more than I ever thought possible. Together, we will convince Bishop Bachman and the elders to accept you as one of our own. After the way you sacrificed your life for me, twice, I believe he will agree."

Hope filled his heart, yet he couldn't shake the lingering doubts. "We must consider *Mammi* Ruth, too. She is a part of this family, and I know how she feels about me. Accepting me as someone you care about, taking Adam's place, will not be easy for her."

"*Mammi* Ruth will learn to accept you, or she won't. I'm not entirely convinced she has really come to accept me, either."

That made him laugh. "Okay, you're right. With love, anything is possible. I'm sure I can wear down her resistance over time."

"The way I have been doing," Elizabeth agreed with a cheeky smile. "Together we will surround her with so much love and caring she'll have no choice but to approve."

"Nice of you to include me in this discussion." A tart voice speaking a mix of English and Pennsylvania Dutch interrupted them.

David turned to see *Mammi* Ruth leaning heavily on the rail as she took the last step. He shot to his feet and quickly crossed over to her. "Take my arm, I'll escort you to the table."

"Denke." *Mammi* Ruth released the rail and gripped his arm tightly. She leaned against him as he guided her to the kitchen.

"Ach, Mammi Ruth, you should have called for help. I would have come to assist, *ja*?" A frown puckered Elizabeth's forehead. "It's nearly midnight. What brings you down so late?"

"I heard the gunfire." Her English was stilted, but he was impressed she even knew that much. It made him realize she'd purposefully excluded him from conversations with Elizabeth.

"I'm sorry you were frightened," David said. "I apologize for the danger, but you and Elizabeth are safe now. The danger is over, for good."

Elizabeth helpfully repeated his words in Pennsylvania Dutch, and the older woman nodded.

"I hear you have put yourself in harm's way twice now to protect us," *Mammi* Ruth said.

He shrugged. "Of course, any man would do the same for the women under his care."

She stared at him for so long that he wondered if her eyes were sharp daggers that might pierce his skin. "You have been a good protector, *ja*?"

He wasn't sure what she was trying to say, but Elizabeth quickly translated.

"God's strength guides me. He watches over His children," David said.

Again, there was another long moment where the elder woman digested his comments. He found himself holding his breath, praying she wouldn't outright denounce him.

Finally, she looked at Elizabeth. "If Bishop Bachman allows David to join our community, then I, too, will give David my blessing."

Elizabeth's eyed widened with surprise, then she impulsively rushed over to give the woman a hug. "*Denke, Mammi* Ruth. Your blessing is *wilkom*."

Mammi Ruth inclined her head. "*Sehr gut. Denke.*"

"Wilkom," David said, grinning widely. He wanted to believe that gaining *Mammi* Ruth's approval would help pave the way for Bishop Bachman and the elders to do the same.

For the first time since he'd known the woman, she smiled. A real, true smile.

He was touched by her acceptance and reached over to take Elizabeth's hand, too.

With God's grace and Bishop Bachman's approval, this would soon be his family, along with Liam and Shauna, of course.

A family he wasn't sure he deserved, but would cherish all the same.

EPILOGUE

Christmas Day

As she worked on the evening meal, Elizabeth wondered what was taking David so long. Liam had driven by earlier to take him on an errand, something he'd needed to get from the Amish Shoppe.

Mammi Ruth sat at the table, cutting potatoes. It seemed that these past few days had shown her mother-in-law that life was too short to hold grudges. Elizabeth knew *Mammi* Ruth would always mourn her son, but she had been surprisingly nice to David over the past few days.

After talking with the local doctor, *Mammi* Ruth had agreed to get up and walk each day, building up her strength. Lying in bed all day wasn't healthy, and likely the result of her being depressed over losing her son. The lack of movement had contributed to her dizziness and falls. The older woman had also begun to help Elizabeth in preparing meals.

"I'm glad Bishop Bachman has already spoken to the elders and all have agreed that David can join our community," *Mammi* Ruth said. "I believe David will begin the process of becoming baptized after the new year."

"*Ja, sehr gut,*" Elizabeth agreed. It was wrong to think of their wedding since he hadn't been officially baptized yet, and since he hadn't officially proposed, but she secretly hoped they would be allowed to marry in the spring so as not to interfere with the planting season.

"Elizabeth?" David came into the house carrying a long wooden board of some kind.

She dried her hands on her apron and hurried over. "*Ach*, what is this?"

"A Christmas gift for you." David beamed, then took her hand in his. "Elizabeth, I love you very much. Now that bishop has accepted my request to become Amish, I would like to ask for your hand in marriage. Once I have been baptized, of course."

She sucked in a quick breath. "Oh, yes, David. I would be honored to marry you. But you didn't have to make me a quilt rack. Just asking is more than enough."

"I wanted you to have a way to display your quilts, and something that would show how much I love you," he said. He gently kissed her, but then stepped back, glancing over her shoulder at *Mammi* Ruth. "A Christmas combined marriage proposal gift."

"David, it's beautiful." She bent down to trace the smooth wood. "It's too much, and I don't have a gift for you in return."

"I don't mind. Hang on, there's more." He went back outside and then came back in, this time carrying a wide headboard. She'd never seen the quilt rack before, but the headboard had come straight from his showroom. He propped it against the wall, then went over to *Mammi* Ruth. "This is for you. I noticed you don't have a proper headboard for your bed."

Mammi Ruth's eyes widened in surprise. "For me?"

"Made by David's hand." Elizabeth was touched by his generosity. "You didn't have to do this. Certain sure you should be selling these to the *Englisch*."

"I know I don't have to do this. That's what makes it so much fun." He took her hands in his. "I understand big, lavish gifts at Christmas isn't the Amish way, but this year I would ask you to humor me. You have done so much for me, Elizabeth, and these gifts for you and *Mammi* Ruth are the least I can do in return."

"*Ach*, David." Tears pricked her eyes at his generosity.

"I'm so blessed to have found you, Elizabeth," he murmured. "Thank you for agreeing to become my wife."

Mammi Ruth spoke in rapid Pennsylvania Dutch.

He eyed Elizabeth, questioning.

Her cheeks heated as she translated. "*Mammi* Ruth has only one request and that is for us to provide her grandchildren." She hesitated, then added, "I was not blessed with children during my marriage with Adam, so you need to know that may not be possible."

"I love you, Elizabeth, and I will also love and cherish any children God seeks fit to provide. My love will not change if God has other plans for us." He dropped to his knee and took *Mammi* Ruth's hand in his. "I promise to take good care of you and Elizabeth. God willing, you will soon be my family."

The older woman patted his hand. "Certain sure you will."

He rose and gently hugged her again. "Merry Christmas, Elizabeth. May this be the first of many."

"Merry Christmas, David." She kissed him again, lifting her heart in gratitude that God had brought them together.

Blessing them beyond words.

* * * * *

If you enjoyed this book, don't miss these other stories from Laura Scott:

Soldier's Christmas Secrets
Guarded by the Soldier
Wyoming Mountain Escape
Hiding His Holiday Witness
Rocky Mountain Standoff
Fugitive Hunt
Hiding in Plain Sight

Available now from Love Inspired Suspense!

Find more great reads at www.LoveInspired.com.

Dear Reader,

I hope you enjoyed *Amish Holiday Vendetta*, my second Amish suspense. I couldn't wait to write David and Elizabeth's story. I visited the Amish community here in Wisconsin and was so impressed with their faith, community and craftsmanship I knew I needed to write a short miniseries about them.

I adore hearing from my readers! Without you, I wouldn't have any reason to write. I can be found on Facebook at https://www.Facebook.com/LauraScottBooks, on Twitter at https://Twitter.com/laurascottbooks, on Instagram at https://www.Instagram.com/laurascottbooks and through my website at https://www.laurascottbooks.com. You may want to consider signing up for my monthly newsletter, too. Not only will you find out when my new books are available (like my next Amish suspense story), but I also offer an exclusive novella to all subscribers, which is not available for sale on any venue.

Until next time,
Laura Scott